The
ART OF LOVE

Printed by CreateSpace, An Amazon.com Company.
Available from Amazon.com and other book stores.

Made in the United States of America
Cover Design: Ennel Espanola
Project Editor: Paulette Nunlee of 5-Star Proofing
Author's Photo: Derrick Pearson of One Way Photos
Author's Make-up: Vadia Rhodes
Interior Design: Milmon Harrison Designs

ISBN-10: 1983749141
ISBN-13: 978-1983749148

Library of Congress Control Number: 2018900644

The Art of Love is Book 4 in the Decades: A Journey of African American Romance project.

The author may be reached at:
SDH Books
P.O. Box 340012
Sacramento, CA 95834
www.sdhbooks.com

DEDICATION

To Briana & Jeline,
My sisters, bautiful & beloved:

I'm so glad Mama birthed me in the middle,
allowing me to be cushioned by both of you on either side.
I can never thank God enough for you. I love you to life!

so vividly. I felt like I was her. Her dreams, her struggle to become successful, and her electrifying passion for a man who was on the wrong side of the law had me glued to every page from beginning to end.

—Tiffani Quarles Sanders,
author of *Unthinkable Sins*

In prose that is almost lyrical, Suzette Harrison's *The Art Of Love* takes you on a sensual journey of romance and danger. Steeped in the era, the passion is palpable and the characters unforgettable. This love affair is a sweet reward you're certain to enjoy.

—Sheryl Lister,
author of *A Touch Of Love* and *Love's Serenade*

Hello Beautiful Readers,

Thank you for joining me in this walk back to the 1930s. *The Art of Love* is the fourth book in the Decades: A Journey of African American Romance series. This series consists of 12 books, each set in one of 12 decades between 1900 and 2010. Each story focuses on the romance between African American protagonists, but also embraces the African American experience within that decade.

I'm honored to be one of 12 authors contributing to this groundbreaking celebration of us. I pray you thoroughly enjoy *The Art of Love*. And if you do, please kindly tell a friend and post a book review.

Here's to happy reading,
Suzette

You can join the Decades' journey on our Facebook page http://bit.ly/2z9sMrd

DECADES:
A JOURNEY OF AFRICAN AMERICAN ROMANCE

January

February

March

April

May

June

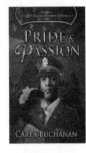

July

August

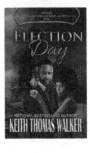

September

October

November

December

The ART OF LOVE

SUZETTE D. HARRISON

CHAPTER ONE
Chase Jenkins

Chase Jenkins nearly lost a load. Focused on the two-party ruckus up the street, a crate slipped from his massive grip. Reflexes quick, he kept the crate from becoming a smashed disaster at his feet.

Better stay your brain on your business.

He chided himself for being inattentive and exceedingly fascinated.

Chase forfeited precious seconds admiring the, oh so, enticing stranger apparently attempting to out-argue a much older man.

Lord in Zion...

From midnight skin to a bold swerve of feminine curves, and healthy hips that flared with a promise of pure pleasure, she was absolutely lovely. And hot as Hades. Even at a distance, her passion was apparent. Her animated gestures were like fierce punctuations outlining her objections. Even so, she was pure seduction; a woman worth his wayward observations. Thoughts of tangling with her wild sultriness, riding deep between her thick thighs caused an instant throbbing below his beltline.

Man, don't stack up on foolishness!

Wanting a woman like that was an idiot's act.

Never one to lose his mind, or waste his time, he heaved the sizeable crate onto one shoulder and quickly extracted his pocket watch with his free hand. Time was tight. The April sun had begun its descent. San Francisco's infamous fog had already begun to roll in. Yet, his day was far from done. When finished with this market delivery, he had one final run for the night.

His jaw hardening, Chase Jenkins stepped onto the wooden walkway knowing the job ahead *had* to be errorless. Leaving his truck idling, he ignored an itch to grab one more glance of the midnight woman. His mind had to be distraction-free for the task ahead. Focus was imperative.

Within minutes, he completed his delivery. His billfold a few dollars fatter, he left a new, but satisfied, customer behind. His powerful stroll the pace of another man's trot, he headed for his idling truck praying the good Lord would hold back time. He had less than truly needed for his precarious journey into the Oakland Hills.

"How can I pay you if I can't go in?!"

A plush voice, seasoned with the south and snapping like a whip, snared Chase's attention. Thoughts of familial duty and the Oakland Hills faded. That same seductive attraction who'd distracted him earlier, did so again.

The midnight beauty and her argumentative counterpart were no longer dueling at a distance. Rather, they stood outside a small storefront on the opposite side of the street, in his direct line of vision. Foot traffic gave the warring parties a wide berth while casting curious stares.

Whatever their disagreement, it had rapidly escalated, leaving the lovely lady losing ground and sliding towards defeat. Her desperate pleading left him wanting to intervene. But Chase Jenkins had his own dire affairs to handle, and needed to keep his nose clean.

Opening his truck door, messenger cap pulled low on his head, he hoisted his body up and in, intent on avoiding a fight that wasn't his.

"Mr. Randolph, *everything* I own is in there!"

The deep desperation in her southern-scented voice caused Chase to look again. The woman's back was to him. Unable to see her face, he read her body language.

That bountiful body stood in battle mode. Like a man skilled with insight into women, Chase saw beyond her armor to a vulnerability that lay underneath. That glimpse of an internal fragility left him feeling something he shouldn't, maybe couldn't. Shaking it off, he shifted into gear and prepared to pull away.

"Take your hands off me!"

His head snapped about. What he saw incited an internal riot. Gear slammed into "Park," door flung open, he mindlessly stalked across the roadway.

A horn blared. He was seemingly oblivious. His focus was solely fixed on the pale offender manhandling her midnight velvet. Without thought, he planted himself between the woman and her aggressor like a mountain that wouldn't move. Chase spoke quietly. Yet, his voice rumbled with threat and authority.

"Where I'm from, we don't mishandle women."

Caught off-guard, the offending aggressor bristled with supposed superiority. "We're not wherever you're from, whoever the hell you are. We're here. In front of *my* store!" the man spat. "And *she*," the man angrily jabbed a finger towards the woman at Chase's back, "can't enter. Not until I get what's due me."

Chase felt the heat of the young woman behind him. He heard her inhale, readying another volley for her war of words. Eyes locked on the man before him, he made a small, silencing gesture meant solely for her benefit.

The woman grew instantly still.

"You're silent *finally*?" the offended man scoffed. "Good, 'cause you have yet to say one thing worthy of being heard. Your being late is your problem. Not mine." He ended his tirade, mumbling to himself, "Serves me right! I'm the fool for being kind enough to deal with you no good, low-life Colored bitches to begin with."

Iciness flushed through Chase's veins. Managing not to slam a fist in the man's face, he spread the flaps of his jacket instead, exposing the pistol he religiously packed. "Whatever your argument, talk to this woman as if she is one," he seethed, his jaw grinding. "And next time you do…it's best you do it without your hands."

Certain the man was a defused threat, Chase turned to the young woman behind him. Laying a hand at her elbow, he gently led her aside. He intended to speak quickly, quietly, but what was lovely at a distance left him abnormally unsteady and tongue-tied.

Up close and personal, she smelled of sweet wonders and secret warmth. Her rich, deep skin—smooth as glass, and silky soft—tortured the palm of his massive hand. But it was her eyes that proved a snare-like trap. Deep. Intense. Chase got lost in the mesmerizing heat of eyes seemingly capable of seeing the marrow and soul of a man.

He cleared his throat before asking, "You alright, ma'am?"

"No, sir, *I'm not*. And can't *nobody* expect me to be when that cracker has everything important to me!" The woman made a lunging movement as if ready to rip something.

Positioning his body as a blockade, Chase locked an arm about her waist and held her so they faced each other, her hip against his.

Leaning towards her ear, he spoke in a low, slow whisper. "Ma'am, I'mma need you to breathe a bit." When the woman continued her anguished argument, he merely nodded. "I understand, sweetheart, but you can't get nowhere cutting up a fuss like this."

Chase watched the woman snatch her hot-as-Hades glare from her adversary to finally, fully levy that penetrating gaze on him. Amused, he watched the woman glide her fiery eyes over his frame, head-to-toe and up again. He felt her shiver when allowing her gaze to reconnect with his.

He denied himself the pleasure of his own quick, but intimate perusal of her liberal curvature. He avoided staring overly long at her lush lips. Chase couldn't afford to be caught or captured. Not when dire, possibly deadly, business awaited him.

Suppressing his body's response to her nearness, he cocked his head towards the brick edifice behind them. "I take it there's business of yours inside that building?"

Her tight, irritated laugh held the slightest hint of musicality. "If by 'business' you mean my *whole* entire God-given life, then yes, honey, there is."

He ignored the odd sensation her calling him "honey" caused. It was neither intimate, nor personal; yet, tinted with the sensual. "The man?" Chase indicated the one standing with a cocktail of fury and fear marring his grizzled, parchment-colored face. "He's the manager...or the owner?"

He witnessed fuel and fire deplete and seep from the woman's stance and frame. Eyes averted, she heavily exhaled. "Owner."

Chase recounted what was already clear. "And you owe him money?"

She nodded.

"How much?" he softly inquired.

Her voice was tight with embarrassment. "Three months' back rent."

"How *much?*" he repeated.

She remained evasive. "All I need is to access that store, get my work, and deliver it to my customer! When the delivery's done, I'll have enough to make up the back rent and pay a few months in advance. But tell me how that's fixin' to happen with Mr. Randolph acting downright uncooperative?"

"He's not the only uncooperative one out here. You still haven't said the amount you owe."

When the woman looked up, Chase saw a storm stirring behind her otherworldly eyes. "You need to know this, because? What? You have the money?" Her laugh was dry-bones brittle. "And if you do, does that mean you're reaching in your back pocket to pay him?" She snorted dismissively. "And you'd do this why? So I wind up owing *you* a debt only being flat on my back can satisfy?"

Her sensual insinuation ringing like a tortuous invitation, he squashed an involuntary thrill and let his vexation have full play.

Releasing her, Chase responded, his voice gritty and thick, "Darling, I've never bought a woman's favors before, and I don't plan to today."

Tight in the jaw, Chase Jenkins walked away.

CHAPTER TWO
Ava Lydell

Ava Lydell felt shamefaced the moment the wide-backed, strong-shouldered stranger stalked off, leaving her rooted where she was. Feeling oddly alone and cold in the shadow of his absence, she tightened her coat against San Francisco's springtime breeze and watched him approach her landlord with uncommon confidence.

He was unlike the Colored men in her small town down-home. Men, like her father, who were forced to swallow their dignity and step from sidewalks and lower their eyes in the company of whites. This man's stride reeked self-assurance, perhaps race pride. He wasn't belligerent. Rather, purposeful, intent, and far from subservient.

Ava experienced a curious delight watching him interact with her landlord as if equals. The pinched and pained expression on Mr. Randolph's countenance contrasted with Ava's inner exuberance. He was blistering, his pasty face showcasing heated dislike for whatever her stranger was quietly conveying.

Mr. Randolph's displeasure had her making a closer, second inspection.

Skin like warm butterscotch, the man was tall, muscular and wide, abundantly good-looking and—unlike most Colored men of their day—not clean-shaven. An expertly groomed beard shadowed his handsome face, creating a definite aura of powerful masculinity that was distinguished, dangerous and delicious. The longer Ava stared, the more she felt a heat in her womanly places, melting her into liquid fire that suddenly wanted sating.

Father, my flesh is foul, but that don't mean I don't need You just the same. Please let whatever this man is saying aid my way.

Ava's prayer was barely prayed before her heart sank at Mr. Randolph's stubborn objections that sliced the air, causing passersby to pause.

Keeping her distance, she ignored nosey folks edging in on business that didn't belong to them. Instead, she silently willed her tall, strong stranger to continue his fearless negotiations. If, in fact, that was his course of action.

And if it is?

Her desperation spiked. She was in no position to bargain. She was a Colored woman in a cold trap of impossible dreams, near pennilessness, and too much pride. Of necessity, she might be required to consider whatever the stranger's asking price.

Just get me back inside.

Mr. Randolph's store held her art. Holding her art was synonymous with owning Ava's life. And her heart.

Ava paced. She prayed. She wanted—no *needed*—something more than frustration, bitterness, and dried-to-dust dreams. She refused to return to Oklahoma, just another broken Colored woman whom life could never love.

Her pacing abruptly stopped when the unnamed stranger beckoned. Masking her face and her fears, she calmly approached both men.

Swollen with self-inflated power, her landlord was quick to reestablish his position. "You have ten minutes. Get in. Get out."

Ava swallowed sizzling words poised to spew from her lips, and spoke as calmly as she could. "Mr. Randolph, ain't no way on God's good earth I can clear everything out in ten minutes."

"You take today's delivery only. You have until seven o'clock tonight to bring me what you owe. That happens? You'll be on good ground and…" Her landlord glanced at the now silent stranger. She caught the look of understanding that passed between them. Nervously clearing his throat, her landlord's tone softened. "I'll let you back in."

Ava's words were a rushing river. "Thank you, Mr. Randolph! I promise—"

"Save your promises. Make that delivery the best way you can and bring me my cash."

"The best way I can?" She stood puzzled. "Your nephew's still driving me, Mr. Randolph…sir. Right?"

"My family's finished helping you, Miss Lydell," the man snapped, removing the padlock securing the door.

Ava clenched her teeth to keep from cussing.

This cracker's crazy!

Short of God sending angels to her aid, moving a massive piece of pottery across town was doggone impossible. She didn't own an auto-mobile. The work was too heavy to transport on her own. And, Lord, knew she didn't have money the first for the trolley or a cab.

Her mother's voice suddenly echoed in her ears. *A cracker's a cracker no matter the address.*

White folks Up North might refrain from parading around, gruesome ghosts in sheets, burning crosses by night and terroriz-ing. Nonetheless, though milder in form than the blatant Jim Crow oppression she'd grown up with, the vileness of California's crackers could certainly burn as bright. While Mr. Randolph was fair as out-west white folks knew to be, she'd already pressed her luck and said more than was prudent. Desperation had left her showing her tail and 'talking out' in ways that, had she been back home, might have left her swinging lifeless from a limb. Like her mama's mother. Taking a deep breath, she cautioned herself to reel it in while contemplating how to achieve a seemingly impossible feat of moving her work across town. Wallowing in her woes, Ava barely heard, "Glad things worked out, ma'am. Good night."

A moment passed before she realized *he* was leaving…and that his absence left her feeling oddly cold, again.

She spun in the direction of the departing man. "Wait, please!"

He turned just enough, leaving her to admire the strength of his profile, the thick deliciousness of lick-able lips.

Ava intuited by his stiff posture that he remained offended by her previous comments regarding his intent. "Sir, please pardon my speaking out of turn earlier," she offered, hurrying to where he wait-ed. "I didn't mean to be vulgar or insulting."

His slight nod conveyed acknowledgment and forgiveness.

"I didn't thank you." She suppressed a shiver when he gazed down at her with unveiled interest.

"You just did." Touching the brim of his cap, Ava's stranger strolled away.

Mesmerized, she stared, foolishly admiring his confident gait and no-nonsense air. His strength was apparent as he crossed over to a truck waiting on the opposite side of the roadway, its signage proudly declaring, *Sylla's Delivery Service.*

Ava felt a thrill, wondering if he was the angel answer to her prayer.

She took off running despite better sense.

"Excuse me! *Sir?*" Ava dashed across the road as her handsome stranger climbed into the truck's cab. "I'm truly aware you've helped me enough already." Her words flowed airy and breathless. "And I don't have much of anything worth your efforts or your time. But, would your kindness allow you to consider helping me once again?"

"Ma'am, your landlord'll let you back in—"

"No, sir, it's..." Ava gripped his arm and her words halted at the hot, electric surge created by their contact. It was the same heat she felt when he'd grabbed her to keep her from murder and mayhem. Instantly, she withdrew her hand, feeling his incredible nearness in ways unimagined. "I *really* need you...or rather, not you...but your truck."

Ava's words raced over her tongue, explaining the situation her lack of transportation created.

When she finished and the man merely stared down at her unmoved, desperation determined her next words. "I'll compensate you *however* you want...or as best I can."

When the handsome one cocked a brow, and a languid, but loaded, smile lifted his full lips, Ava absolutely regretted her hastiness.

CHAPTER THREE
Chase

Introductions made, Chase knew her name. *Ava.* It was the song of a gentle wind. Having witnessed her in action, he decided she was anything but. Ava Lydell was pure hurricane.

He'd watched her take a flat-footed stance against a white man and—his aid, aside—win. She'd turned one victory into two by effortlessly roping him into loading her work onto his truck where she rode shotgun as he completed her delivery while foolishly pushing his own business aside. All by the sheer power and pull of those penetrating eyes, the sultriness of her scent…and the sweet sway of voluptuous hips.

These hips alone are persuasive!

His pace was purposefully slow. He allowed an excited Ava to hurry ahead, granting himself the chance to admire the backend of hips that had him choked for time, and hot below the beltline.

Lord, ain't much sweeter than a Colored woman's curves, Chase allowed. No overt skirt-chaser, he'd never wanted for companionship, had languished in the forms of his fair share of females. But this here woman's figure was…

Art, Chase decided. *Plain and pure.*

"Mr. Jenkins…"

Chase and his hot perusal were forced to a halt when Ava spun in his direction. "Chase," he corrected. "'Mr. Jenkins is my granddaddy, and he's dead."

"And your father?"

"What about him?" He unsuccessfully harnessed the snap in his comeback.

He saw her stall, her lovely head cocking sideways. "A man typically references his daddy with that kind of reply."

"Guess I'm not typical, and my daddy ain't worth the reference."

His silent stare dared further intrusiveness. He felt a sense of relief when she merely shrugged and resumed her initial line of thinking.

"I wanted to thank you again…for everything. This couldn't've been done without you," she admitted, waving towards the large, pristine home they'd just exited.

Chase had played his role to perfection, providing the muscle power she needed to safely deliver her pottery, then standing discretely aside as her business was transacted. On the other side of success, the silent tension that enveloped her on the ride here had evaporated. The joy on her face indicated her patron had been pleased, had paid in kind, and her money was in the black again. When she opened her pocketbook and withdrew several bills, his countenance darkened.

Ignoring the money Ava extended, he proceeded to where he'd parked.

"Hold on, now, Mr.—I mean, Chase…"

The sweetness of her purring his name, had him pausing and allowing her to catch up.

"Take it. Please."

Chase sidestepped Ava and her money. He was caught off-guard when she thrust herself in his path, cutting him off from his truck.

"Since when does a Colored man decline greenbacks?" Her laughter was free and rich as she slapped the money against his chest. "Honey, midnight ain't but a minute."

"Meaning?"

"Hard times ain't never far, and quick in coming. You better take this."

Enjoying her relaxed mood and unexpected closeness, he looked down into luminous eyes that appeared able to see and know his soul. His hand nearly swallowed hers when covering her fingers resting against his chest. Enticed by the softness of her skin, he held on a moment too long before stepping forward, minimizing the existing space between them.

He removed the money from her hand. Inching even closer, he felt her shiver, the accelerated rise and fall of her full breasts against his chest as he slid the currency back into her open pocketbook.

He lowered his already deep voice, allowing his words to flow like gentle waters against her ear. "I don't need your money, Miss Ava Lydell."

He smiled at her cautious, tremulous, "What do you need?"

He found pleasure in torturously whispering, "Something sweet… spicy…and satisfying."

When she took a backwards step, he snaked an arm about her

waist when she teetered slightly. "Careful, there."

He didn't bristle, but merely smiled when she shook him off.

"What*ever* you want—sweet, spicy, or otherwise—you best get it from your women friends. I'm not a gumball machine. I don't dispense."

His grin was suddenly teasing, sensuous. "I don't want what I want from another woman, and I sure can't get it from nobody's machine. What this man needs can come from you and you only."

"Pardon me?"

He lifted his hands in mock surrender. "Miss Lady, I'm simply calling you on your offer to compensate me 'as best' you can," he explained. "And, trust. What I want is best…for us both."

He laughed outright at her obvious indignation. He leaned back and crossed strong arms over his wide chest when she flung words at him, one hand planted on a curvaceous hip.

"Lemme educate you here and now, *Mr.* Jenkins. You got me mixed up and mistaken for the wrong kind of Colored woman. I don't—"

"Bake?" Chase inserted.

"What?"

The sun had set. The prime time for his own, private business in the Oakland Hills was nearing an end, and there he stood playing with a woman? Something about Ava Lydell made him want to stay where he was, enjoying her presence, uncovering more of her essence. His smile mischievous, Chase advised, "You owe me, and I've decided your payment is a sweet potato pie."

"Come again?"

"You're familiar with them?"

"I know what a sweet potato pie is."

"That's how you're compensating me. With some down-home deliciousness." Chase couldn't help adding, "What'd you think I meant?"

"Nothing," she mumbled.

"Oh yeah, Miss Lady, you thought *something* and it wasn't Christian or clean. You standing up here calling my character into question, *again*. So…since you feel the need to insult me twice, make it two pies and we'll call it good."

He liked the way her grudging smile blossomed into full bloom, enhancing the deep brown of her satiny skin. "What makes you think

I know anything about pie-making?" Ava questioned, turning towards his truck.

He reached past her to open her door before standing back to slowly savor her top-to-toe, his eyes resting, feasting on her well-fed curvature.

Ms. Ava, those hips say you know yoour way around a kitchen.

"I appreciate your doing for me, but I don't want you having to cart me all the way back to the shop. I'm sure I can catch a cab somewhere out here."

Chase glanced from the roadway to Ava seated beside him. Fresh and feminine, she looked out of place in his delivery truck. Still, she felt right. As if she belonged wherever he was.

He refocused on the road, determined to ignore the rightness of her presence.

He had the same need for women as most men. He'd simply never let need exceed the bodily. His mother had, and his father had misused and abused her love, grinding her down to dust. Abandoned, his mother had been left with five children, her husband's debt, and heartbreak that never healed. He'd learned the pitfalls of living in love by watching his mother: he knew to guard his heart like a prize.

"You've done plenty enough for me, and I can't take additional advantage of—"

"Where're you from?" he interrupted.

"What makes you think I'm from anywhere but here?"

He smiled slightly. "Too much down-home on you for you to be a purebred California girl." Chase chuckled outright when Ava replied,

"Honey, I ain't seen girlhood in a month of Sundays, but I'll take the compliment."

The sun had set. Night had come. Streetlights were rare on the uneven strip of passage that was becoming more rugged and rural as they traveled. That didn't keep his eyes from straying her way. "Miss Lady, you're barely a taste over twenty."

Ava's pure laughter rang like music in his ears. "Mr. Jenkins, I'm not a woman ashamed of her age. I'll have you know, I saw the last of my twenties three years ago."

He refuted her claim. No way was this satin-skinned woman four years older than him. A challenge on his tongue, his words were lost, never spoken as a force fiercely slammed into them.

A crushing sound of metal against metal scraped the air. He gripped the steering wheel, struggling to correct the vehicle's front end. What control Chase gained was ripped away with a second impact that sent them wildly spinning in the opposite direction. Protectively, he sprawled his body over hers as the truck churned and swirled, and swayed violently sideways before righting itself again.

Hearts pounding in sync, he found himself atop of her, unable to enjoy pleasurable sensations for the danger of the situation they were in.

His words were a rushed, hushed whisper. "You okay?"

Caught in shock, she merely nodded.

The sound of feet pounding gravel had him hurriedly lifting himself from her and reaching into his waistband.

"I need you on the floor," he ordered, gun instantly in hand. Seeing her comply without sass-back, Chase knew she understood they'd encountered more than an accidental collision.

Helping her assume a crouched position, he instructed, eyes like steel, "Stay there unless I come for you."

Inhaling, Chase prayed a hasty prayer before kicking his door open. He dropped flat to the ground, gun drawn.

"Rum Money!"

Ignoring the scratchy-voiced summons, he focused on scoping as much as possible from his vantage point via the aid of headlights illuminating the night.

"You might be bright-skinned," the seemingly disembodied voice continued, "but you didn't disappear! Face up, Jigaboo, if you don't want these boys coming in with a vengeance."

He eyed four men stealthily approaching within firing range.

Outnumbered or not, he was tempted to unstrap the rifle hidden in a hollow well beneath the truck bed. He'd swallow the odds and take his chances...but for precious cargo. Placing his passenger in peril wasn't prudent or on his agenda.

Whispering so softly he hoped she heard, he cautioned again, "Do *not* move."

Hating a defeated position of surrender, he slowly stood.

"Put whatever you're packing on the hood," the scratchy voice demanded.

Arms stretched wide to the side, Chase complied. He stepped into the open, intentionally drawing attention to himself to keep the focus from where Ava hid.

He didn't flinch when men rushed him. He tightened his frame against the first two hammering blows that bent his body in half.

Exhaling through clenched teeth, he ignored the burning pain when righting his posture. For Miss Ava's sake, he made the hard choice to not strike back, to not reach for the pistol at his ankle, to avoid a bloodbath. Eyes hot and piercing, he used what light the stars provided to mentally catalogue the faces of Domino Garamelli's men. He promised himself he *would* see this crew again. For now, he had to contend with this moment when his dark and deadly business in the Oakland Hills had snuck up and come for him.

CHAPTER FOUR
Ava

Ava's heart was a runaway locomotive burning through her chest.

There was nothing arbitrary about this collision. It felt orchestrated, planned. And far too dangerous for Ava who was pinned in a cramped, crouched position—barely breathing, absolutely unmoving.

Danger was no stranger to Ava. She'd migrated from the deep pit of Oklahoma where racism reigned. Where Colored folks lived life knowing their circumstances could drastically change between sunrise and sunset. It had for Ava's family.

Her grandmother, a woman of God's gospel, had been strung up despite her piety. With her grandmother's lifeless body swinging from a tree, it was difficult to decipher whether her murder was initiated for sermonizing Colored folks' rights...or calling Prohibition a divine denouncement from God, and preaching against the "sin of liquor" and the moonshine peddling of a certain clan of white men in their backwoods community. The horror of her uncles cutting down her grandmother's mutilated corpse all those years ago still occasionally crept into her sleep, making nightmares of her dreams.

Positioned as she was, Ava felt the similar threat of danger steal over her. She saw nothing, could only catch snatches of discourse. Whatever fear she should've felt was swiftly replaced by indignation as she pieced together the raw, coarse conversations of men.

Rum Money?

How had Chase acquired that name? And what did he owe these men that he obviously refused to give?

Intuiting that money was at the heart of the matter, she prayed Chase wasn't pocket poor. She fervently prayed he had whatever he owed, and that he would give it and end this unwanted interlude before it escalated in further violence.

Prayer unanswered, she flinched, hearing the impact of flesh against flesh. Chase's resulting grunt left Ava feeling sick, as if thrust back to Oklahoma all over again.

"Check his truck!"

She tensed as another blow landed in sync with the scratchy-voiced command.

"Check the bed. Tear it up if need be, but find my damn money!"

Ava held her breath as feet pounded her way, as men clambered onto the truck bed, causing it to rock with their frenzied search for hidden matter that proved nonexistent.

"There's nothing here," a voice called.

"Look in the cab, stupid nigger!"

Being an inch away from discovery flushed cold liquid through her veins. Still, she was eerily calm, composed when quietly snapping her pocketbook open. Without hesitation, Ava extracted the switchblade kept for protection's sake, slid it into her coat pocket and waited.

Their eyes met and held the moment Ava was gruffly pulled from her hiding place. The descent of night did nothing to hide Chase's rage as he stood in the clutches of two men, physically constrained.

"Rum Money, whatcha hiding here?" Scratchy Voice asked, walking to where she stood, a stooge clutching her arm, a gun against her neck. "You running a new line of business?" The man, whose voice sounded like he snacked on gravel and glass, walked around her making an open assessment. "Rum Money, you taking to running women versus whiskey?"

She jerked away when the white man's clammy hand gripped her face. She stiffened as he laughed and turned to look at Chase. "She's good looking enough…if you don't mind sinking your stuff in dark meat."

Her mouth flew open with a ready retort. A quick glance at Chase stalled her midway.

It was nearly imperceptible, the cautionary shake of Chase's head. Ava saw. She understood. She said nothing, clenching her teeth and locking hot words beneath her tongue. She focused on Chase.

She followed the downward flicker of his gaze.

In the encroaching night, she saw nothing. Save a slight protrusion that was ankle height.

"Check her! See if she's holding my funds."

The barked order was immediately obeyed.

Her hijacker laid hands on her, searching out the unseen. She protested as he moved from toe to top, obviously enjoying the deed. When his paws settled on her breasts, she turned without thought. Ava let loose her best when punching him.

Male laughter ripped and rolled as the man staggered back.

Recovering his footing, he came for her.

"Touch her and a bitch is burying her boy."

Stillness was instantaneous. No one moved.

Eyeing the circumstances, Ava knew she and Chase had stumbled into a lions' den. There were five men to their two. Even so, with the deep of his voice rumbling through her, she knew his threat was anything but idle. The scratchy-voiced one obviously knew it, too.

"Just do what I told you without all the extra!" he yelled.

One hand holding his wounded jaw, the man finished searching Ava only to come up empty-handed. Gun trained on her, he supplied, "She ain't got nothing."

Without a word, the goon leader slammed a fist against Chase's midsection.

Ava inhaled sharply.

"Where's my damn money!"

"Wherever the hell it is," Chase grit out, earning himself another hit.

"Stop it!" When the man ruthlessly pummeled him once and yet again, she acted.

Reaching into her brassiere, Ava quickly detached the small pouch holding the money she'd just earned. She flung the pouch to the ground like filth. It sprawled forlorn…along with her dreams and hopes. "There! Just take it, but *stop hitting him!*"

Too important to stoop or bend, the ringleader instructed one of the men holding Chase to retrieve what Ava had discarded. She watched the man count the earnings of her art beneath the bright light of God's moon.

"Seventy-five bucks," he announced.

It was by far the most she had ever earned on one piece. It was enough to pay her studio rent in arrears as well as supplement her meager salary from the diner to, hopefully, keep her afloat until her next work sold.

By the man's scoffing expression, she knew it wasn't enough to settle up.

"Nothing but a drip in piss," he growled, pocketing the money and giving Ava his full attention.

She wanted to scrape the lecherousness off his face at his slow inspection.

"Tell you what, Rum Money. I'll take this dark meat with me."

She was immediately grabbed by the man she'd earlier punched. Her protests failed when his pistol pressed painfully against her ribs.

"You want her back?" Scratchy continued. "Hand me what's mine and we'll make an exchange." Posturing in Chase's face, the man compromised. "Better yet…how about I let her earn what you owe? I can line up plenty men who like spreading night-colored thighs. She's got solid hips that'll give a *good* ride."

The goon assigned to Ava chuckled. "You ain't never lied."

"You want first run, Poundsey?" Scratchy inquired.

Affirming he did, Poundsey slid the gun down her thigh—his opposite paw grabbing her belly and inching south towards parts that weren't his.

As if an involuntary action, Ava reached into her coat pocket. Switchblade in hand, she brought it down deep and hard across her captor's arm.

His agonized howl tore the air as he fell to one knee in pain, cussing her to hell and back again.

Attention whipped Ava's way, granting Chase opportunity.

She never saw a man move quite as fast.

In the confusion the injured idiot created, Chase broke from the men holding him to reach the firearm at his ankle. He came up, pressing the pistol directly against the ring leader's head.

His deep voice was a quiet slice in the night. "Here's your sole option and exchange. We leave. You live."

She heard Chase's gun cock when one of the men moved to challenge him. She took to praying.

"Guns on the ground."

She was slightly stunned when the men reluctantly obeyed. Who was Chase "Rum Money" Jenkins to sway outnumbered odds in his favor? Or was it a mere matter of sparing their leader's life that caused them to comply?

"Miss Lady, get your pocketbook."

She quickly retrieved it from the truck.

"Fools, kick those guns towards the lady and back the hell away. Miss Lady, you a good aim?"

"No," Ava lied, feeling the instant warmth of his slight smile.

"How about you target those tires and get some practice in?"

She quickly retrieved the surrendered firearms. Placing them in her pocketbook, Ava hurried towards the vehicles that had collided with them. Swapping guns when the first was emptied, she set about destroying both sets of tires until gunshots echoed and faded in the empty night, leaving a stench of hot metal behind.

Turning towards Chase, she experienced a tiny thrill at the surprise and admiration lighting his eyes.

One arm around the ringleader's throat, the other holding that gun steady against his head, Chase pivoted, walking slowly backwards towards her.

"Miss Lady, climb on in."

She quickly complied, reaching across to secure the driver's door open for him.

She inhaled sharply when he made the man kneel. "Lord, please no." Despite the insults against her person, she prayed Chase wouldn't escalate the violence. They'd already gone too far and done too much.

She exhaled with relief when he backed himself up and onto the seat beside her, leaving the man to live. Within moments, the engine revved to life. They sped away and disappeared into the arms of night.

Knowing she'd shot out tires, making them useless, didn't keep Ava from glancing over her shoulder, hoping to not find vehicles in hot pursuit.

Shaking feverishly, she jumped when Chase reached across, placing a calming hand on her arm.

"Ava. You alright?"

She felt an electric shock. At his touch. At the intimacy of her name on his lips without a preceding "Miss".

"No...I'm not." A hand at her stomach, she pressed the other against her mouth hoping to suppress a rising torrent. "Pull over, please."

She made it outside just in time to put distance between herself and the truck's lone occupant.

On the side of a near-deserted, unpaved road, Ava heaved, hunched over, spewing the only meal the day and her quarter-dollar afforded.

"Take this."

She heard and felt his gentleness, the kindness of his huge hand flat against her spine.

"I'm fine." *And proud. And ashamed at being this kind of helpless before a man…*when her mother had taught her to be steel-backed and self-sufficient.

"I beg to differ, Miss Lady. Take it."

Righting herself, she accepted the checkered handkerchief he offered. Wiping her mouth, Ava smelled his subtle cologne in the cloth she held. The scent was masculine, delicious, and mixed with the essence of a handsome but hazardous man.

"Who are you? And what was that foolishness?" She flung an arm in the direction they'd just fled.

"Something I'm sorry you had to witness."

"I did more than 'witness', *Mr.* Jenkins! I contributed!"

Standing in the dark with him, her chest felt tight, tense. She'd left down-home, intent on immersing herself in art and leaving bloodshed and violence. Here she'd met, and been forced to rely on the largess of a perfect stranger, only to find herself in an unwanted world, again.

"You did fine," Chase reassured. "You did what was needed in the moment. No one was hurt—"

"I nearly cut a man's arm off!"

"You left him alive. No one walked away dead," he joked with a grin.

She couldn't suppress the small, relieved laugh sputtering from her lips. She couldn't catch the thrill, or keep it from spreading beneath her skin as he stepped close, smoothing a strand that had somehow strayed from the marcel waves crowning her head.

"You left something important back there."

"Such as?" She questioned, wanting to—but unable to—move away from his uncomfortable closeness.

"Money hard-earned."

She was instantly freed from his enchantment.

Angrily, Ava moved towards the truck. Locating her pocketbook, she dumped the emptied pistols onto the truck bed before scrounging its meager contents, searching for a mint to combat the sourness caused by her retching.

"Better hang on to as many mints as you can, Ava Lydell," she muttered. Thanks to her lost earnings, that handful of mints might prove her supplemental nourishment in the lean days ahead.

"Ava."

She turned at his voice. She was disturbed, again, by his nearness. She felt his warmth despite the cool, fog-drenched April air.

"It's all I have right here and now, but it's yours."

She allowed him to press a folded bill hidden in the gun holster about his ankle onto her palm. Ava indulged his closing her hand over the money, and covering her hand with his. "Is it dirty money?"

"Clean or dirty, it won't make up for what you lost. But, hopefully, it'll help make do."

"I'm so sick of living like my Mama gave me 'Make Do' as my middle name when she never did."

His bold laughter was unexpected. As was his sudden wincing in pain.

Ava went instantly into action. "Take off this jacket."

"No need, Miss Ava. I'm fine."

"Tell that to your crumpled up face," she snapped, seeing him wince again. "I can patch you up," she decided when he cooperated, removing his work shirt tucked in his dungarees, "but I need better light. You're gonna need to come with me."

She was gentle when helping him dress. Her voice was brisk when asking, "You bootleg?"

Despite knowing the answer, she sighed when he confirmed, "I'm a rum runner, yes, ma'am."

CHAPTER FIVE
Chase

C hase didn't mean to deceive by allowing her to believe his injuries were deeper than they were. God knew his midsection felt on fire, but he'd experienced worse. Right there and then, he simply needed to prolong the pleasure of Ava's tender fingers against his bare skin.

How hands that had expertly handled a gun could now soothe with an angelic touch, proved a tantalizing phenomenon.

Her ministrations were gentle, yet certain. Conveying her understanding of a man's flesh and form. She touched his body as if he were art and she was artist, repairing damage done.

"I know it stinks to high heaven, but it'll help minimize any bruising."

He wrinkled his nose at her mixture of sage, lard, and something dark and pungent that she refused to identify. "I smell like sausage on Sunday."

The musicality of her short-lived laughter was sweet. Other than providing directions, she had been stubbornly silent on the ride to this little diner that had become their makeshift medical clinic.

He didn't fault her for her stillness. He'd subjected her to an ordeal that was potentially deadly, and unquestionably terrifying. While she had handled herself flawlessly, he viewed tonight as a reminder of why he couldn't afford a woman in his world. His living was too often perilous, and the stakes too high. Yet, Ava Lydell possessed something that made him want to unload his risqué burdens and rest his head in her lap long enough to live whatever life love had in store for him. As if singed by flames, he backed away from the thought.

"Ice would help with any swelling, but the ice man doesn't come 'til morning," she explained, tearing cheesecloth into wide strips.

He nodded, keeping his arms aloft as instructed as she wound the strips about his solid torso with caution and care. From his perch atop a rectangular table against a wall in the small diner's equally modest kitchen, he felt hypnotized by the clear intensity of her eyes as she

tightly secured each cloth strip with safety pins. When she offered
to send a jar of her homemade salve home with him, he opened his
mouth with a ready decline of Ava's sausage-smelling solution. Instead, he flinched with real pain at her accidental pin prick.

"I'm so sorry." She unwound the cloth to examine his skin for
possible punctures. "I didn't mean to poke you." Her concern was
medical, her touch magical.

Chase's jaw tightened at the torture of her fingers stroking his
abdomen. He laid his hand over hers, stilling her gentle care. "Miss
Lady, I'm fine."

"You sure?"

"I been pure punched in my gut tonight. You think I'm worried
about your little pinch?" His voice grew edgy, speculative. "You gotta
mister somewhere who'd object to you touching me like this?"

Her laughter was short, brisk. "If I do I haven't met him yet."

"Good to hear." Inwardly, Chase chided himself for seeking un-
offered information, for wanting to know if she was available to him.
He hurried away from idiotic divulgence. "Why do you have a key to
this place?" He indicated their surroundings with a lift of his bearded
chin.

"I waitress first shift." She efficiently, carefully reaffixed the cloth
bandage. "Usually, I'm already prepping tables long before the cook
arrives, so it makes sense for me to have a key instead of acting like an
alley cat and waiting out back for someone to let me in."

"Why waitress when you're an artist?"

"It's a means to an end."

"Would you prefer doing your art versus wasting your time here?"
he persisted.

"This 'waste' puts meat in my mouth."

"Point taken. But if given a choice would you wash your hands
of this and do your art exclusively?" He watched her looking oddly at
him.

"In case you haven't noticed, Chase Jenkins, it's the 1930s and
we're living in the hungry hands of a Great Depression that ain't
fit for a Colored woman's fantasies." She shrugged nonchalantly.
"Besides...the diner's only open for breakfast and lunch. Which
explains why it's closed now. Getting evenings to myself gives me a
fair amount of time for my craft. Is it ideal? No, sir. I'd rather spend
every day, all day in my passion Still...my morning may start with me

doing what I don't want, but I end my nights doing what I love. Life is what it is."

Chase experienced a hot jolt, imagining days and nights submerged in *her* passion, making slow love to her until neither could take any more. Images of Ava, nude as nature, sprawled decadently beneath him—meeting him stroke for stroke—roared through his mind with unexpected heat and surreal poignancy. He felt his groin quickening.

"Why do you run rum?"

His heat and hunger took a backseat to her questioning.

Eyeing her, Chase slowly slipped his arms into his shirt and pulled it over wide shoulders. "To continue your thought, sweet lady—Depression or not—this country's never had room for a Colored man's wants. Prohibition made space."

"Prohibition as in '*prohibited*'. Bootlegging's illegal, Mr. Jenkins."

"According to the Ten Commandments, so are a lot of other vices, but that never stopped white men from committing them. White men don't want me in their offices except to clean." He touched her chin. "They don't want you in their dining rooms except to serve them. They want to prohibit and prevent? That's fine seeing as how I don't much enjoy their company to begin with. Like I said, smuggling liquor provided space and created a way. White folks making liquor illegal was one of the best things that could happen to an enterprising Colored man."

Chase enjoyed the aggravated sway of her hips as she went to wash her hands at the sink. "So you being a bootlegger and running rum is a race thing?"

He grinned despite her obvious irritation. "Whether it is or not, to quote you, it's a means to an end."

He watched her dry her hands and turn her back to the sink, arms across her full breasts, studying him. Chase cocked a brow when she dropped her arms at her sides and marched forward. He didn't move when she withdrew folded bills from her brassiere and thrust them at him.

"I don't touch whiskey—or anyone who does—on account of white men stringing my grandmother up for preaching for sobriety and against Prohibition. Thank you, but I don't want it."

He looked down at the money wadded in her hand—the same "make do" money he'd earlier given. "Might not want it, but you need it."

She stood unpersuaded.

He sighed. "Sweetheart, that ten dollars was earned from today's market deliveries. It has nothing to do with hooch, moonshine, or white lightning. It's clean."

"Maybe, but I'm not keeping it. I already owe you for helping me deliver my pottery."

"And we already decided that's a debt sweet potato pies can settle and satisfy."

He said nothing when she stuffed the money in his shirt pocket, patting his chest with finality.

"I can't owe you anything, Chase Jenkins."

He grabbed her wrist when she turned to walk away. "If anyone owes anyone, it's me. You lost your earnings tonight because of being in my company. Like I said, I *will* reimburse every dime those ignorant asses stole."

"Technically, it wasn't stolen, honey. I gladly gave it just to keep them from hurting you."

That said, she turned and left the room.

Chase didn't realize his hunger until spying the cakes lined atop the diner's counter beneath glass domes. He hadn't eaten since a breakfast of ham, eggs, potatoes and grits. After tonight's ruckus, he was ravenous.

"Might as well increase my debt by five cents," he mumbled. Finding a saucer, he served himself a slice while contemplating the night.

He'd embarked on a run designed for retribution, only to land in a spider's web. He wouldn't fault Ava for bringing his guard down. The blame was his. And his brother's blood remained unavenged.

He was on a second serving of cake when he felt her re-enter the room. Looking away from his impromptu meal, he found Ava in the doorway. Face soft and damp, the fresh scent of mint, perhaps toothpaste, gently wafting, he presumed—that after her roadside upheaval—she'd freshened up in the diner's restroom.

"I can make you a cup of coffee to go along with that stolen cake if you like."

He chuckled softly. "No, ma'am, I've already added a dime to my debt."

"You plan on getting away from here?"

He paused eating his sinfully-delicious, butter yellow cake with fudge frosting meal. "Ma'am?"

"The men who were after you tonight: how do you propose escaping them?"

Placing his fork on his plate, he gave her his full attention. "What makes you think I would?"

"Those men weren't playing, Chase. They may be dumb, but they're dangerous."

He shrugged. "My granddaddy always said, 'a man who's right doesn't run'."

"Not to contradict your granddaddy, but sometimes a man needs to leave to lengthen his living."

He flashed a grin, before growing serious. "The men we encountered tonight are cowards who're fool enough to think I'll conduct my business like them: tail tucked between my legs, running back where I come from—"

"Which is?" she interrupted.

"Southern California."

"Migrated from down-home?"

"My parents came up from Louisiana, but me…" He shook his head. "Born and bred."

"Is southern Cal your rum-running territory?"

Chase nodded. "It was."

"Was or is?"

His gaze narrowed. "Miss Lady, you're asking a lot of questions for a woman who ain't interested. Any specific reason for your asking?"

He watched her shift her weight from one foot to the other before quietly answering. "None that I can imagine." Chase smiled when she contradicted herself by continuing. "So…you're not heading back to southern California. You'll stay here?"

Elbows atop the table, he linked his fingers before his mouth—his thumbs stroking the underside of his bearded jaw while watching her watch him. His heart rapped a beat, finding in her penetrating eyes something mildly illicit, yet inviting and sweet. "That's up to you."

"Me?"

"I'll make a way to stay for one gun-toting, beautiful, chocolate-brown woman."

To Chase, her laughter felt hollow and insincere. "I'm not the decision-maker for a stranger, Chase Jenkins. I don't know you."

"You could."

"Doesn't mean I should."

Slowly pushing away from the table, he strode across the small space to where she stood in the kitchen doorway staring up at him. Running a finger over her smooth cheek, his voice deepened. "You could, and *most definitely* should."

Before she could respond, he had an arm about her waist. Pressing against her, he did what he'd wanted since first coming face-to-face with her earlier that day. He leaned down intent on just a teasing taste.

He should've known better than to play. The mere touch of her lips proved intoxicating, dangerously provocative.

Captured, he maneuvered her backwards, pinning her against the doorjamb. Testing. Tasting. The smooth depth of her kiss, the lusciousness of her lips.

His mind told him to pull away. A more powerful force compelled him to flat out remain. To savor what Ava skillfully gave.

He shivered as her hands did a slow slide up his back to stroke his neck. Something excavated itself from deep within his chest when her soft mouth opened and allowed him in. He groaned at the touch and torment of her tongue, and the flavor of her brown sugar deliciousness.

Their tongues mutually pursuing, his hands strayed to hips that had, from the start, tantalized and tempted.

Lord...Jesus!

Raw hunger hit him full force below the belt as he palmed the sensuous scope of her hips, wanting to spread them wide and slip into the heaven they hid.

Chase felt inexplicably cold when Ava pushed him away.

She spoke as if breath didn't come easy. "I need to get home. And you need to leave."

He refrained from touching her again, knowing if he did there'd be no leaving until he'd tasted and seen her everything.

He took a necessary moment to recollect himself. "Lock up. I'll take you home."

"Actually, you won't."

His head tilted sideways as he studied her, trying to discern the impassive look descending like a mask over her visage. "Is there a problem?"

She straightened her dress, needlessly smoothed the near immaculate marcel waves she wore.

He felt a hot flash of hunger when she looked at him, finding his own heated desire reflected on her face.

Ava dismissively advised, "No need for you to know where I live."

He watched her swish away, her sultry scent lingering behind, testing his strength to abstain.

"This is 'so long and farewell. Negro, get out my life and good-bye'?"

Her laughter rang pure. When she grabbed her pocketbook and turned towards him, her face was like flint. "I sincerely thank you for coming to my aid and helping me cart my art to my customer. However, Chase Jenkins, after a night with you, I'm flat broke again."

His rebuttal was interrupted by Ava raising a halting hand.

"Somehow I'll fix the situation I'm in. But I have no plans to ride Bonnie to your Clyde. I hate violence and bloodshed, and will *not* be in a mess with a hazardous man." She slipped on her coat. She was finished.

Chase caught her elbow when Ava would have sashayed past him. "I promised you before that I'll make good on getting every dollar back that was taken tonight."

"Good to hear. Come 'round tomorrow afternoon, and I'll have those sweet potato pies waiting on you."

Disliking her nonchalance, he stared hard into her eyes. Her indifference had him speaking without thinking. "I'm also promising you here and now, Miss Ava Lydell, I'm not going anywhere until we get what I want and what *we* need."

"And that is?"

"Me tasting all of you…and you doing likewise. Top to bottom, baby."

Snatching up his jacket and cap, he left—angry, pride bruised—that a woman he'd known less than a day had burrowed bone-deep beneath his skin.

CHAPTER SIX
Ava

Midnight was a memory, yet she lay sleepless, doggedly examining various angles for reprieve from her predicament. Thank God, she'd heeded her mother's advice to "keep a little piece of something" until her art proved profitable. To that end, she had willingly worked whenever, wherever The Depression permitted paid labor to appear.

Thankfully, she had the diner to help fill in the gaps caused by a lack of art sales. Unfortunately, her shifts at the diner had been reduced to a bare minimum. Most folks didn't have extra to dine out with The Depression leaving dry bones where plenty had been.

Where earnings failed, the church was prepared to step in. A practical man moved by compassion, her pastor had established a Benevolence Society to assist those stricken hardest by hard times. She, however, had no intention of taking what was meant to serve the elderly, or families with children. Nor would she expect aid from Roosevelt's National Recovery Act that served white folks first and Coloreds, maybe, next. Colored folks didn't rename the N.R.A. the Negro Removal Act for nothing. The slight had merit.

Rubbing a hand over her face, a cash-deprived Ava was no longer high on hope. With abject resignation, she admitted that envisioning herself an accomplished artist wouldn't pay her way, and dreaming was a dusty pursuit at best.

She sat up from the floor palette that served as a makeshift bed. Pressing her back to the storeroom wall, she wearily stretched her legs and examined her hands. Only constant care allowed them to escape the proof of her young years as a washerwoman.

You paint real fine, Ava, but you're wasting time doing things not meant for you and your kind. Be content with your lot and don't strive above your station.

The words of the white woman who'd intermittently employed her had cut like daggers, but they also propelled her to escape limitations and dreariness. Putting all her hopes in coming up north, or *west*, she'd dared to believe she held the power to recreate her existence. Six years had passed since she'd traded Oklahoma for dreamland, and she had yet to savor sweet success. Her career as an artist had been an unwanted series of hits-and-misses.

"Shoulda stayed in New York," she quietly lamented, thinking how the Harlem Renaissance had provided a birthing place for the Talented Tenth—that creative body of Colored authors, playwrights, and varying artists.

Harlem proved a hot bed, a place where Negritude exploded with great fanfare. Yet, in specialized genres, the dominant often only "permitted" room to a few—as if Colored art should be monitored so as not to exceed imagined limits. While Ava readily credited both women with inspiring her to brazenly open her own studio, Augusta Savage had already satisfied America's Negro sculptor market, and Edmonia Lewis had taken Europe by storm. In painting, artists Aaron Douglas and Archibald Motley, occupied the top leaving little room for the Avas of the era.

Unquestionably gifted, Ava could sculpt. She could paint. But, not having a benefactor had proven detrimental to the solvency of her craft. Patrons were particular, and The Depression made investors wary and overly selective.

Hearing that tolerable racial relations existed out west, she'd left New York for San Francisco's art district in a circuitous migration. Riding the train through Bakersfield and Fresno—California's drylands—she'd witnessed Colored folks in the fields picking cotton as if time and place stood still. Yet, she'd pressed on praying she'd find more room for inclusion in the ocean coast's art community along with better opportunities. Certainly, she'd enjoyed impressive successes, but nothing that catapulted her to a place of notoriety or fortune. After years of struggle, Ava faced destitution and a decapitated dream.

Stomach sour with the bitterness of defeat, she stood and walked the silent hall leading to the diner's restroom.

The diner's bathroom was remarkably clean only because Ava kept it to her liking. Managing it dutifully was part of her pretense; a way to erase evidence of public usage while negotiating her homelessness.

Washing her hands, she spoke to her mirrored image. "It's hardly ideal, but I'm grateful."

But for grace, she could be—like so many others—solely reliant upon soup kitchens. Or sleeping in abandoned railroad cars, or ditches. Instead, she secretly found safety and sanctuary in the small utility room at the back of the diner.

Chase's stalking exit had saved her from unnecessary pretense. His leaving first made it unnecessary for her to walk the block, waiting for him to disappear before returning to the cramped room where—unbeknownst to the diner's owner—she slept.

Avoiding detection, she slept here while storing her belongings in the rear of her art studio.

"You mean what *was* your studio," Ava reminded her reflection, trying not to cry over the seventy-five-dollar blessing snatched from her hands that very night.

Sighing, she sat on the closed commode, dreading sunrise and having to stare bitter consequence in its evil eyes.

Knowing Mr. Randolph's cracker ass, he's probably already put my things on thse street.

Her lovingly painted *Art by Ava* sign that she propped in the front window every afternoon. Her paintings. Pottery. More than the state of her affairs, the idea of her art being tossed curbside as if forsaken children, abandoned and unloved, reduced her to heart-wrenching sobs.

Cool water soothed. She splashed her skin yet again.

Eyes closed to the dripping liquid, Ava blindly fumbled for her towel, fingers encountering damp material instead. It was Chase's handkerchief, the one offered roadside at her intestinal woes. She had hand-washed it and spread it to dry. Bringing the cloth to her face, her nostrils were—despite the laundering—immediately treated to the masculine beauty of him.

Lord, that's a pretty man!

She'd fought to focus while tending his wounds. Even now, her fingers tingled as if imbedded with memory of him. His wide shoulders and broad back. The musculature of his solid torso and chest. She'd gently applied salve to his tender places while wanting to know the taste of his warm butterscotch skin, the weight of his body on hers, the length of him buried deeply within. Fanning a flush of heat, she forced her thoughts away from traps of the flesh.

Instead, she saturated her mind by replaying the loss and danger of the night. Her vanished funds. Her emptying a gun like some

woman from the Wild West despite her fear. God *knew* she was
thankful they'd walked away from what could've been as her mind
revisited every twist and turn...only to circle back to that man, again.

Man?

"Twenty-nine!" She snickered. "He's a baby, is what he is."

Ava's mind stubbornly insisted he was a 'youngster' off limits
despite the fact that her body knew something different.

San Francisco's fog was slow in relinquishing its reign. Like
spun cotton, its damp tendrils clung to the dawn, dancing slow and
hypnotic. While cold mornings like this made her miss the heat of
Oklahoma, she was often seduced by fog's sultry dance. But not this
day. Impervious to its seductions, she hurried through the smells and
sounds of daybreak.

Approaching the small, familiar flat, Ava—out of habit—looked
for Lurlene's signature signal. Finding the flimsy slip of material tied
about the doorknob, she sucked her teeth.

"That scarf's spent more time on that door than it has Lurlene's
neck." Her predicament had her knocking despite the scarf's presence
signaling an implicit agreement. Her former roommate would be
irate, but she could care less.

She was forced to knock several times before hearing footsteps on
the other side. When the door was snatched open, she encountered
what she expected. Dressed in barely-there underwear, a disheveled
Lurlene looked and smelled like she'd been busy on her backside.

"*What the hell, Ava?*" Yanking the scarf free, Lurlene angrily waved
it in Ava's face. "You broke *and* blind?"

Ava pushed aside the silky signal representing their tense, tacit
agreement that she would not disturb when her former roommate
was "entertaining".

"Lurlene, I'm not in the mood for you and whatever pecker-
wood's pecking between your widespread legs. I need your help, so
get dressed."

"Help?"

Ava stood, unperturbed by her friend's disdainful laughter and
indignant stance. "I done already told you how to work up on some
fast money, Ava Lydell. But last I checked, you were still too good to
lay on your back."

Ava exchanged a long, heated glare with the roommate whose

abode she'd left when Lurlene opted to turn their dwelling into a makeshift brothel for her constant stream of "paying friends." Having met on the train whisking them west in search of better, she'd grown to love Lurlene despite disagreeing with the woman's methods of earning an income. She had—after fruitless conversations—simply removed herself from their once-shared residence. Lurlene's uncle owning the flat, gave the other woman preeminence. Despite their fall-out, for Ava, Lurlene was still more sister than friend.

Their sisterhood had Ava softening. Playfully, she patted her own behind. "Honey, this here is priceless."

Lurlene's laughter was raspy thanks to damp morning air and the newest supplement to her Depression-altered diet: home-rolled cigarettes. "Get your crazy self in here! Bugging me at this godawful hour. Whatchu want? A shower? Thought you used the common bathroom over your studio."

"Lurlene, that's not why I'm here—"

"Well, how much money you need?"

"None," Ava answered, stepping into the dinky, dank space Lurlene insisted on calling a 'parlor'.

"Ava, don't forget who you talking to. I know you broke as Satan on Sunday."

She raised her hands in a declining gesture when Lurlene reached into a brassiere struggling to make her bountiful bosom behave. "I don't want none of your hoochie-nasty-coochie money, Lurlene Sims. Just come help me get my things before that fool landlord of mine sells them."

Her first impression when meeting Lurlene six years ago on that westbound train was that the woman, two months her senior, was edgy and excessively ready for living. She had watched The Depression and life out West transform that edginess into unbridled boldness.

Lurlene's ribald tales of the men she entertained, had Ava laughing loud and long as they walked arm-in-arm through San Francisco's morning mist. "Lurlene, hush with all that! Got me out here acting unseemly too early in God's morning."

"Ava, Lord knows I'm telling the truth. Here he was this big ole thing standing over six feet! I knew fo' sho' he was packing meat. *Humph*! Honey, he was going to town…"

Ava swatted Lurlene's arm, halting her friend's crude, rude hip-thrusting.

"…just a-huffing and a-puffing like he was making me sing. When I didn't feel no pleasure in my parts, I told that man to hold on while I got up and got my magnifying glass to see his thing."

"You lying ten ways to Sunday, Lurlene Sims," Ava managed on a laughter-broken breath.

"Maybe, but I got your mind off your troubles for a minute."

Squeezing Lurlene's hand, Ava fell silent.

You can always go home again.

Home to what? she wondered. Sharecropping "can see to can't", managing a rickety plow and a half-dead, mangy mule? Helping her parents who, despite being near fifty, birthed a new baby bi-annually? The oldest of eighteen, Ava had already given enough of everything. Even her mother cosigned and agreed.

Baby, follow your art. Go'n somewhere away from here, and dare to do.

Forbidden to return to school by her father after completing the eighth grade, Ava had been assigned a life of plowing, planting, and helping raise her siblings. Ava had saved art solely for herself. *She* alone owed herself an opportunity.

She knew she'd offended Chase with her stubborn refusal of his financial assistance, but fierce independence was her sole treasure.

Baby, don't never *take nothing from a man. Don't give too much, neither. You do, you'll be fixed in bondage. He'll own you!*

Her mother's words cycled softly through her, despite Lurlene's loud-talking. Images of the women in her family, her small town community, filled Ava's memory.

Many strong had been weakened. Some were penniless, or solely dependent on the earning ability of their men. Striving. Sharecropping. Their female beauty dimmed by sowing and hoeing rows of Oklahoma soil beneath a seething sun. They were put upon by the demands of life, men, and children. Even her own mother—eighteen offspring later—was a raisin-like rendition of who she once was. Saving little for self, her mother unguardedly gave away her essence and strength.

"Keep your independence," her mother repeatedly insisted, determined her daughters would avoid the mistakes she'd made. Defying her husband, she'd pushed Ava to seek her own way—fighting for her daughter when she couldn't for herself.

Ava had taken the teaching to heart, protecting herself and her pursuit of art. Saving every penny she could from washing white women's clothes, she—with her mother's help—fled Oklahoma the first moment possible. Her father had been irate learning of his oldest child's "abandonment." Though empathetic, Ava was unapologetic. She *had* to live in a world not corralled by mediocrity, countless babies she could barely feed, and plowing the land of white men. Choosing lavish dreams, she felt like a fraud faced with eviction from her studio and the loss of space in which to freely create.

Acting crazy with Lurlene couldn't camouflage the terror of Ava's heartbeat. Nearing the intersection, she prepared herself to round the corner and witness the decimation of a dream. A clean walkway had Ava halting, her steps faltering, wondering why her life's love hadn't been upended.

Gripping Lurlene's arm, she practically ran them both across the street to her storefront of a studio. Finding nothing out of order, she dared to believe God had honored her tear-soaked prayers.

Ava's hope spun the opposite direction, finding the salon door ajar and Mr. Randolph there.

"I changed the locks last night when you didn't show as agreed," he informed as she tentatively stepped inside. "Now, I'll have to charge you for a new key."

"Sir?"

"Don't 'sir' me, Miss Lydell. You should've been here like you promised, and spared me unnecessary changes!"

She was confused hearing Mr. Randolph's rant, but seeing the stingy pleasure on his face.

"I went and promised some remote relative of the wife's that he could rent this space once you vacated. Good thing I don't like him. I won't feel bad reneging. Relation or not, it's only right you keep the space with so many months paid in advance—"

"Pardon me?" she looked at Lurlene standing silently near the entry, her face sharing Ava's profound confusion.

"You might be paid up for the next six months," her landlord slapped one palm onto the other, "but come month seven, your rent's due again, and I *will* demand payment in an on-time fashion!"

"I don't understand…"

"On-time's the opposite of late and lackadaisical, Miss Lydell. You folks do comprehend that, right?"

"Us folks comprehend wanting to cut your cracker a—"

Ava hurriedly silenced Lurlene's unsolicited comeback. "I'm referring to the prepaid rent, Mr. Randolph. What do you mean my rent's paid six months in advance?"

She felt unsettled by her landlord's look questioning the voracity of her sanity.

She watched the man grab a dark brown envelope trimmed in gold from atop the modest stand dedicated to her window display. Ava accepted the sheets of paper thrust her way.

"There's the typed notice you had delivered, along with my handwritten receipt."

Ava read and reread both. She stuttered, shaking her head in disbelief, "I-I didn't type this, Mr. Randolph. This…this letter…whatever money you received…it-it wasn't from me."

With a disinterested shrug, the landlord extended Ava a new key. "Might be from the man on the moon. Doesn't matter." He laughed heartily. "You have your studio back, and I have my money."

"The money was hand-delivered?"

"Yes, Miss Lydell," her landlord replied irascibly. "By some blond-haired boy. Good call on your part. All that cash might not've made it had you sent it by some Colored kid."

Feeling Lurlene puff up at the insult, Ava grabbed her hand.

Despite further questioning, all Ava could ascertain was a blond-haired child had delivered the envelope containing what amounted to six months' rent late last night before leaving via automobile with a white man.

The matter made no sense. Ava couldn't wrap her head around it. A great God had looked down from heaven and used some unknown white patron to divinely grant a Colored woman's anxious petition?

The windfall blessing exceeded her experience. With Mr. Randolph's departure, she said a prayer for the unknown patron she couldn't thank. Grabbing Lurlene's hands, Ava danced a quick jig. "Nothing this good ever happens to a Negro woman from piss-poor Oklahoma!"

"God must be different out here, out west," her friend chimed back.

Slowly walking about her studio, viewing her work through eyes brightened by blessings, Ava silently thanked her private patron for—in Lurlene's words—sparing her from "selling tail and skating through hell."

Letting loose a wild whoop like women back home in Oklahoma when "catching the Holy Ghost" in their open-air, dirt-floor church, Ava experienced something she hadn't in a long time. She felt hope.

CHAPTER SEVEN
Chase

He told himself to stay away. To forget Ava Lydell's sensuous form, the sweetness of her lips and hips, and the heaven in her visage. Despite such self-caution, he found himself headed in the direction of the diner with the collecting of sweet potato pies his legitimate ruse and excuse.

Last night's mayhem with Garamelli on his mind, thinking her disposition might be more salty than sweet, he armed himself with a gift and peace offering.

Finding a rear table, Chase ordered black coffee with sugar. No cream.

The diner's two-for-one Thursday special generated a steady hum of business activity that afforded him a needed opportunity to covertly watch Ava in action.

The more he watched, the more intense the need. He'd wrestled it throughout the night. Now, in the light of day, severe need confronted him boldly, directly. Far from virginal, he was no stranger to bodily satisfaction. Yet, he'd intentionally refrained from anything remotely like a relationship. And he certainly never had, never would chase a woman anywhere for anything. Until now. Until this inexplicable, inescapable thirst came calling. He wouldn't deny wanting to taste and touch her spirit, her soul, as well as the lush fruits of her physical being. Sipping hot brew, he capitulated to an incessant idea: how to make Ava undeniably his?

She'd become fire for his flesh, a need that burned beyond belief. He wanted that woman like he wanted life's force and energy. The magnitude of his need was foreign and strange, as was his relentless crave to repeatedly make love to her until they were both deliriously depleted.

As if drawn by the hot magnetism of his thoughts, he saw Ava turn in his direction. Plates in hand, she stopped.

He allowed his heated gaze to convey the, oh so, private place his mind had been. His lips lifted in a scandalous grin when she cocked an eyebrow and walked towards the kitchen, ignoring him.

"Excuse me, miss..." Chase hailed the only other waitress.

"Good morning to *me*." Sizing him up, the woman all but purred, "Honey, I can sho' 'nuff get you what you need."

"Miss Lydell...the other server...mind asking her to stop by?"

"Honey, I'm more than happy to keep you and your coffee hot."

He grinned at the woman's open flirtatiousness and suggestive expression. "I don't doubt it, but I'm only needing one woman to top me off. Miss Lydell, if you please." Chase hid his laughter in his cup as the woman smacked her lips before sulking to the kitchen.

He wasn't forced to wait long. Ava appeared momentarily, bearing a pot of fresh coffee. The worried woman from the prior night was gone. Ava looked peaceful, refreshed. "Chase," was her pleasant, but one-word greeting.

Unable not to, he let his gaze wander her feminine form. "Miss Lady, that uniform doesn't suit you, but the look on your face is lovely. You seem recovered from our personal and private adventures last night."

She glanced quickly about. "You need to say such things so loudly?"

He feigned innocence. "What's the problem, Miss Lady? We did or didn't share an intimate, eventful evening? You had my shirt off, and your healing hands on my naked skin as I recall."

"Chase Jenkins, I'mma fool if I stand here playing with you."

When she turned away, he was instantly on his feet, maneuvering himself to block her retreat. "Let's start over again, and try with niceties. Good morning, Miss Lady."

He felt something soften inside when she awarded him the full radiance of her smile.

"Morning, Chase. You okay? Bruised up any?"

Placing her hand on his midsection, he slid a little sensuous into his tone. "I'm still hard...and healthy. And, no ma'am, no bruising. What about you? Sleep okay?"

He grinned at her staring open-mouthed as if stuck, at her pulling her hand from his body as if burned before answering.

"Didn't sleep a wink. Had too much on my mind."

"Including me?" he teased.

"Everything but. I prefer sweet dreams."

His chuckle was belly-deep. "Fair enough. Your first experience with me wasn't worthy of a lady's evening. I come bearing a tangible apology." Retrieving the peace offer deposited on his seat, he presented her with a solitary rose the color of rich, sweet cream.

Chase felt the internal shift of something inaccessible when Ava gingerly accepted his gift, staring tenderly at it as if the bloom were imbued with sentimental message and meaning.

"It's *beautiful*." She paused to inhale the delicate fragrance. "Thank you kindly."

Nodding an acknowledgment, he saw a sly, playful look move across her face.

"Chase Jenkins, are you cheap or just have no home-training?"

"Ma'am?"

"This rose is gorgeous enough all by itself, but seems to me it's lonely for missing eleven friends."

He leaned towards her ear, whispering seductively, "A dozen requires you accepting an invitation to certain things not suitable for saying in mixed company." To his surprise, she didn't react with indignity. Ava flowed with his playfulness, whispering in return,

"Baby boy, you wouldn't know what to do with my dozen-kinda loving." Ava moved past him to refresh his cup. Voice at normal volume, she kindly inquired, "More coffee, sir? Cream? Sugar?"

Chase resumed his seat, looking at her intently. "Cream, no. Sugar, yes. I like hot things that pass my lips to be dark and sweet."

"I'll say," was her only comment.

Blowing into his cup, he asked nonchalantly, "You busy tomorrow evening?"

"Depends."

"On?" he asked.

"What, why, and who's asking."

"You like jazz?

"Love it."

Chase pulled a folded flier from the pocket of his overalls. Spreading the flier open, he handed it to Ava and waited while she read— enjoying the widening of her eyes and the blooming of an awestruck smile.

"How did I not know about this?" she asked, crushing the flier against her breasts. "Leigh Jones in the Bay Area?"

"One night only," he stated. "You know her music?"

"Do I know her music? Honey, like I know my name. Her "Love's

Serenade" is legendary!"

"I take it, you like?"

"Enough to spread butter on that woman's bread!"

Chuckling quietly, he sat enjoying her out-of-character gushing.

She was nearly breathless when virtually singing, "Her "Love's Serenade" is like digging through a treasure chest of dazzling gems and coming up with raw diamonds." Bracing the table with one hand, she leaned toward him, nearly whispering. "I ain't one to brag… but a few years back a young gentleman bought one of my figurines. Turns out he was jazz pianist Miles Cooper. Next thing you know I'm getting a 'thank you' card from Ms. Leigh herself on account of his gifting her that figurine. I still have that card, and I've been a fan ever since."

Noting the warm blush in her deep brown cheeks, Chase made a simple, salient observation. "You're passionate."

Lifting the solitary rose to her nose, Ava inhaled and countered, "About art and good music, most definitely."

Lowering his voice, he leaned in. "About love…and loving?" Chase felt something unlatch itself and roll through him at the warm, loaded look she levied.

"That remains to be seen, doesn't it?"

"I'm all for seeing and experiencing."

"Begging your pardon?"

Chase removed the flier from Ava's grip. Laying the paper on the table, he held on to her hand. "I'm requesting the pleasure of your company in seeing Leigh Jones tomorrow evening."

"I've experienced enough of you to know you're not right for my nights, Chase Jenkins."

"I've apologized for last night's havoc, haven't I?"

"Doesn't mean I want to take a chance going anywhere with you again."

Lifting her hand, he gently kissed it, letting his lips linger longer than necessary. "What if I promise you that the only dangerous thing you may experience is your own awakening?"

Finding delight in the warm tremor he felt in her flesh, Chase's smile bordered on smug, until she bent forward, placing her lips against his ear—turning the flow of their mutual heat back onto him.

"I'm wide awake, Chase. Ain't *nothing* in me sleeping."

That burn that he'd come to associate with Ava sizzled and sauntered through his lower region. He sat inert and speechless as she patted his face and smiled demurely.

"Sit tight, baby boy, and I'll bring the pies I promised."

He left the diner in angry disbelief.

Returning with pies and his freshly laundered handkerchief, Ava had declined his invitation to accompany him to the Fillmore District for a night of Leigh Jones and the sensual sensation of jazz.

"With a half-assed excuse," he muttered to himself as he proceeded towards the next stop on his delivery route.

Chase Jenkins, you're four years my junior.

And that makes me a child, Ava?

No, honey, it doesn't. It makes you too young to be my man.

He left the diner accompanied by bitter irritation.

Who was Ava Lydell, and why the hell had he fallen off his diligence, unlocked some part of his internal being and opened himself to her access?

He needed to shut that internal door again.

Everything within him told Chase that sealing off that place was best. That Ava would only cause him to relinquish power and position that would leave him limp, nearly lifeless. Without much effort on her part, she could make him utterly useless.

The weighty truth of unfinished business still looming over his head, he told himself that staying far away from this fire-eyed woman was in his best interest.

Brown's Ballroom was busy, its at-capacity crowd a testament to The Fillmore's thriving Colored community.

Dubbed "The Harlem of the West," San Francisco's Fillmore District was vibrant, brimming with culture and populated by a Negro community of varying socioeconomic classes. While its creation was a consequence of segregation that refused to stay in its down south cradle, with pride, it was frequently noted that many of The Fillmore's markets, services, pool halls, and theaters were Colored-owned. The Colored community had fashioned in The Fillmore a haven and mecca for themselves.

While The Fillmore's plethora of churches dominated on Sundays, the jazz and blues clubs laid claim to the weekends. Folks fell out dressed to the nines, ready to shine. Hair conked or pressed. Smelling good. Prettied up with face paint. They dined and drank and danced to the music of famous artists who often played white-only supper clubs, only to flock into The Fillmore after their sets, seeking the familiar comfort of their own. Brown's Ballroom proved a favorite place for Colored acts to land. Count Basie. The Duke. Louis "Satchmo" Armstrong. Bennie Moten. Lionel Hampton. Billie, Ethel and Ma Rainey. Autographed photos of each lined the entry, proof of their stopping by Brown's to sprinkle their magic on the crowds.

Brown's Ballroom was nightlife with an upscale touch. Unlike The Fillmore's hole-in-the-wall speakeasies where knife fights, crooked card games, and drunken love spats decorated the nights, Brown's was sophisticated with its live orchestra, hat-check girls, uniformed hostesses, and easy jazz. Peace was reinforced by the presence of burly "gentlemen" strategically stationed like sentinels throughout the place and at the front doors. Thanks to Chase, Brown's furtively served some of the best liquid spirits in town. With Colored folks occupying every table and seat, only his monetary investment in the establishment allowed his entrance.

"Man, we gonna have to hold up a wall."

Chase surveyed the crowded establishment, concurring with his companion as they squeezed into the back of the dimly lit room. "Thought you said you'd sit butt-naked on a roof in the rain to hear Leigh Jones sing?"

"Man, I ain't here to hear her sing. I want that woman to inspire my next naked dream."

Their laughter leaped before settling. Hailing a cocktail waitress, Chase ordered a tonic water with lime, contradicting his role as a rum runner.

He enjoyed the occasional, cold draft, but never touched hard drink despite having spent the majority of his adult years running risks and covertly supplying hard liquor to those who did.

Sipping tonic water, he had to admit a certain predilection for the danger of it.

He enjoyed the rush and thrill. Being his own boss, conducting his own business. Besting the game, and outsmarting federal agents and other white men. The required stealth and negotiations. Bootlegging could often be a matter of diplomacy and iron will. Unfortunately for Chase, the game got too painfully real...and his brother was dead as a result of it.

He downed the remainder of his drink, his head tossed back. Cool liquid soothed the sorrow clogging his throat, still his heart felt lacerated. A year wasn't enough to forget he'd failed in his role as driver, while his brother served as the front man. A year was too long to not have uncovered the culprits responsible for his brother's death. But he'd come closer than close.

But for Ava.

Had she not been present, he might have the blood of men on his hands.

Lord forgive him, but he would have used all force necessary to dig truth from that cesspool, Domino Garamelli—the scratchy-voiced bastard and Chase's primary suspect. Not only had the man encroached on his Southern California territory—destroying a delivery and outing Chase's activities to authorities—he was certain Domino was directly involved with his brother's death. Domino was a conniving, thieving, moral-less murdering bastard at best.

When I finish with him, I'm finished.

Peering about the smoky room, he admitted the end of his enterprise. His industry could take him the duration of Prohibition, but without his brother by his side, his business operations no longer held the same attraction or shine. Chase was tired of dealing with unscrupulous individuals. He'd tired of living outside the law. He needed something more, something that didn't tax his soul or his mind, a different kind of satisfying.

You need the love of Ava.

He snorted.

"You alright, Rum Money?"

Chase glanced at his companion. "I'm good." He chuckled lightly before asking, "How's that arm?"

Lifting a heavily bandaged appendage, his companion cursed before laughing. "She near 'bout chopped it in half, but it's hanging on here."

"Yeah...I didn't see that coming."

"It's the trickiness of the trade. Whatchu gonna do with her?"

Chase stared at the man keeping him company. Their being together in public was unwise, but Brown's was a safe place and sanctuary. "I'm doing nothing."

"Deny it if you want, but you already into something. It was plainer than day two nights back: that hot chocolate woman has you."

Discounting the observation, Chase swirled his empty glass.

"Play blind if you want, Rum Money." The man laughed. "You'll see."

Noncommittal, he decided he needed a refill.

"Ain't but three servers in here. You gonna either use your clout, or push your way to the bar and wait a while."

Preferring a low profile, Chase didn't misuse his investment and partnership in Brown's superfluously. He could walk to the bar like any other somebody. He headed to the bar needing a cold draft to override memory's bitter dredges, and a woman's witchery…

Maneuvering a sea of humanity, he slowly made his way, stopping short of the bar when encountering a familiar scent.

He scanned his surroundings, thinking he'd fooled himself into her presence. With the press of bodies about him, it seemed illogical that he should detect her fragrance. Yet, he did.

"Sir, can I get you something?"

Shaking off the sensation of Ava's invasion, Chase stepped forward, placing his order. Hearing the emcee opening, he turned his back to the bar to direct his attention center stage. That's when the bottom fell out, leaving him in a daze.

She was mere feet ahead, her back to him, seemingly searching the room until a seated woman waved a hand.

Ava returned the greeting, and Chase ignored his ridiculous relief that she wasn't there in the company of some other man. Instead, he indulged himself with the sight of her navigating the crowded room, oblivious to his presence, lovely as a flower in full bloom.

He suppressed his initial instinct to make himself known. Drink in hand, Chase moved to the shadows to enjoy his illicit advantage of watching Ava, unseen and in secret.

Even Leigh Jones was hard-pressed to command his attention.

His back to the wall, Chase gladly spent his time vicariously enjoying the music via the emotions captured in Ava's profile. The chanteuse and her sultry sounds became mere backdrop to his fascination as the night wore on.

This is senseless.

Never had he allowed a woman to affect or impact him in such a manner. Part of him felt resentment. The other throbbed with dangerous discontent. The more he watched, the more he wanted.

Just once…

Chase chuckled at his own foolishness. He already knew once wouldn't be enough. If he tasted Ava, he'd want her twice, ten times… possibly for life.

Placing his mug atop the bar, he summoned the hostess peddling cigarettes and sundries. Quietly conveying his request, Chase patiently waited, eyes on Ava—the rum-runner in him ready for the risk.

CHAPTER EIGHT
Ava

She felt bathed by a shower of sultry notes and sensual jazz. Music moved her almost as much as her art, touching the tender, hidden parts that only artistic expression allowed her to convey. She felt soft, fluid. Limitless. Like she could sculpt and create a world of beauty in one breath.

Eyes closed, she sat, her newly polished nails tapping the tabletop in rhythmic agreement with the live music.

"Excuse me, miss."

Eyes opening, Ava looked up at the hostess she'd earlier noticed strolling the room with her tray of wares: smokes, chewing gum, roses for big spenders, carnation corsages for those low on funds.

"This is for you," the woman informed, offering a single cream-colored rose. "It's from the gentleman near the bar."

She spun in her seat. Had he chosen to attend despite her declining his invitation? Ava scoured the area behind them, fully expecting to find Chase. She was uncertain whether her heart pounded in disappointment or relief when finding the bar empty of his presence. "Who sent this?"

"Oh my...I apologize," the hostess offered. "He was just right there."

"Girl, you in here charming men without pulling off your panties?" Lurlene's laughter rankled as Ava looked about, this time unable to deny her disappointment.

"I don't see him now, but the gentleman did ask me to give you this."

Taking the folded note from the hostess, Ava opened it and read:

Two down towards a dozen.
C. Jenkins

"Ma'am, I don't mean to be a bother, but the gentleman arranged for me to deliver a flower every five minutes until the job's done. Is that okay?"

"That's…fine," Ava murmured, thinking Chase Jenkins half-way crazy, or fully insane.

"I need to take a page from your book."

She looked at Lurlene sipping her cocktail all dainty and ladylike. "Lurlene, I haven't offered this man a thing, so don't credit me yet."

"It's from the same man who helped you with your delivery?"

She simply nodded.

"Honey, ain't too often a Colored man's willing to act *this kind of fool* for a woman. Best sit back, take it all in, and enjoy it while you can."

Forty-five minutes later, she sat with the borrowed vase the hostess had been kind enough to provide, ten roses richer. And, yet—despite furtively searching—she found no sign of the man.

She managed to focus on Leigh Jones providing an extended performance for her sole stop in northern California. But as that final five-minute interval wound down without the prompt appearance of the hostess, she forgot about the magic of music, wondering instead what new game this man was playing.

Where are you, Chase?

She had already used one visit to the ladies' room to furtively scour her surroundings in search of him. She refused a second trip and playing into his hand. Sighing dismissively, Ava considered the possibility that Chase had left Brown's Ballroom.

Ballroom?

She shifted in her seat, taking in as much as she could of the wide, low-lit space. While the décor was decidedly muted, Ava had to admit gutting the upper level of the old Victorian was genius. What remained of the second level was U-shaped flooring wrapping three sides of the building—creating a balcony overlooking the main stage.

She had only frequented Brown's twice before, but never the second floor exclusively reserved for high-cotton customers.

Her spine tingled as if warm fingers slid intimately down her back.

The second floor?

Inhaling deeply, she took her time turning and slowly looking up.

Everything in Ava went still, finding Chase staring down at her, his expression one of decadent devouring.

Bowing gallantly, he stood at the wrought iron balcony, the final rose in hand.

"Lurlene…" Ava nudged her companion, discretely motioned up.

"Bless the name of Jesus," Lurlene moaned upon seeing Chase for herself. "That's *him*?"

Eyes on Chase, Ava nodded in the affirmative.

When he made a beckoning gesture, she told herself not to move, to make him suffer for his game-playing. Her body betraying, answering his invitation, Ava stood and headed in his direction.

"I'll be back, Lurlene. Hold my seat."

Lurlene chortled before muttering, "Honey, you done with me for the evening."

The seduction of roses reduced her to virginal inexperience while mounting the stairs.

Nervously, Ava patted her perfectly-coifed marcel waves, praying an unappreciated bout of jitters would settle itself and disappear. Without vanity or conceit, she reassured herself of her appearance. Her freshly bathed skin sweetened by a hint and mist of the special toilette water normally saved for Sundays, she smoothed the borrowed, glittering ankle-length gown better suited to Lurlene's smaller frame over her flesh. Grateful to have worn the pair of stockings she'd splurged on and kept wrapped in tissue paper for special occasions, Ava—despite her nerves—suddenly felt oddly luxurious. Thoughts of wishing for a looking glass to confirm that what she felt was indeed what she was, vanished when finding Chase waiting on the landing above the top step. His hungry expression was looking glass enough.

"Miss Ava Lydell, the artist." His voice seemed deeper, his shoulders broader in the cut of a tailored tuxedo that fit him more than fine. It was a stark contrast to his delivery uniform, and evidence of his rum-running success. "For you."

Ava accepted the final rose, and his hand, feeling like a treasure beneath his warm gaze that traveled her length and sultry width, apparently missing nothing.

His remaining where he stood, versus moving back as she mounted the final step, landed them chest-to-chest, her face lifted to his.

"Did you follow me here, Chase Jenkins?"

"Would you let me catch you if I did?"

The nearness of him unleashing unfathomable sensations she'd rather not feel, Ava stubbornly admitted, "Seems like I'm already caught."

"That you are," he concurred, sliding an arm about her waist.

Her body flushed with anticipation at the unveiled appetite in his gaze. "What do you want, Chase?"

He took his time responding. "Nothing but to know you."

"What do you need to know other than I'm a dirt-eating, country gal tryna piece together a dream?"

She shivered when he placed a lingering kiss on her shoulder not covered by the straps of her gold-tone slip dress. Ava gritted her teeth against the heat blasting her being when his lips moved to her throat, Chase whispering,

"Does that dream have room for me?"

She fought for an excuse.

Chase was dangerous. He was a twenty-nine-year-old youth. Hadn't her mother repeatedly told her to find an older man who didn't want much beyond a hot meal and the occasional feel good? Yet, the moment she met him, Ava knew Chase was more man than she was accustomed to. And as a man he'd flawlessly seduced her, rose by rose, while waiting unseen in the shadows of Brown's Ballroom.

He spoke quietly in between suckling her throat. "There's more to Ava than I can see. Tell me who she is."

She took a steadying breath and pushed him away. She examined him long and hard before taking his hand and leading him down the steps.

He stopped her midway, turned her towards him. "What're we doing, Ava?"

Her smile was sweet and sultry when answering, "I can teach better than I can tell."

CHAPTER NINE
Chase

Helping her from the cab, Chase quickly paid the fare as Ava preceded him to her studio.

Impeded by the dark of night, Ava—roses cradled in arm—stood fumbling with lock and key when he eased in close, embracing her from behind to kiss the nape of her neck.

He felt her shiver in his arms, despite her chiding, "Be a gentleman instead of a distraction."

Chuckling, he took the key from her and successfully unlocked the door, letting them in.

"Wait while I find a light so you don't bump into nothing."

He paused at the threshold, waiting and wanting. To blend his body with hers. To hear her southern drawl thicken with heat and hunger. To make love to her until the sun rose on their flesh laying sprawled and exhausted.

"Welcome to *Art by Ava*," she sang, holding aloft a lit hurricane lamp that illuminated the interior of the small storefront serving as art salon.

After her previous reluctance regarding his knowing where she lived, he didn't question her bringing him here. Rather, he accepted the gift of her graciousness. Yet, admittedly, he was curious about the use of the lamp versus electrical lights, concluding perhaps it was her way of heightening romance. Vaguely, he was aware of her finding an empty container for her bouquet. These matters were mere flashes on the backdrop of his mind as Chase stood in the doorway, the wonder within the room possessing his true attention.

His previously helping Ava had involved meeting her at the backdoor to quickly load an already crated piece of pottery prepped for delivery. Here in the soft light of night, he marveled at an unveiled and impeccable gift.

Paintings, sculpted pieces and pottery of plaster and clay in varying stages of completion dominated the small storefront. The undeniable beauty apparent in each testified of creation by the same hand. It was a beauty that rendered him momentarily speechless.

"Lemme take your hat and overcoat."

Handing her both, he slowly walked the room, inhaling all he could of Ava Lydell, the artist.

Bathed in lamplight, her art was an extension of her intrinsic self. He felt her use of color—its vibrant hues, and muted tones. Fingering pottery pieces, Chase sensed her touch lingering like love. There was passion, purpose, depth and breadth, fragility and strength. Her art was a window to the woman. Ava's artistry was an enchanted net reeling Chase further in, leaving him awestruck. "All of this is accomplished right here on the premises?"

"All but the firing," she answered, explaining that in exchange for painting a mural for the family-owned Italian restaurant two blocks over, she was allowed to use an old brick oven housed in their alley to fire and glaze her pottery.

He shook his head in wonder, doing his best to take it all in. "And you did all of this...by your sweet self?"

"You think I didn't?" she playfully sallied back.

He moved to where Ava stood, hands on her hips. Placing his over hers, he slowly redirected their hands over her hips to the sweet wonder of her high, round behind. "No, I don't." He kissed her collarbone. "I think you had help from heaven." Kissed the other.

"That, I did," she softly admitted.

"I'm no expert," lifting her chin, he kissed the side of her neck, "but I'd venture on saying your work is immaculate."

Her warm sigh fluttered against his face even as she freed herself from his embrace. "Honey, the only thing I know immaculate is the Lord's conception, and *this* ain't that."

Her provocative tone rolled through him, stoking his already existing blaze. He hungrily trekked her lowering window coverings, and securing the shop door before sauntering his way. He made no objection when she stopped before him, removing his tuxedo jacket and loosening his bowtie. "Not that I'm complaining, but you got a reason for undressing me, Miss Lady?"

"Teaching and training," she answered, lowering his suspenders before unbuttoning his shirt and divesting him of it.

Chase grinned at her visual enjoyment of his form only partially covered by the A-shirt underneath.

"Don't know what kinda course you offering, baby, but enroll me." Sliding arms about her, he bent, intent on her lips, but she backed away from his reach long enough to grab the hurricane lamp.

"Patience is part of my process." Accepting her outstretched hand, he followed as she invited, "Come with me."

Curious, Chase allowed Ava's leading him to what proved to be a rear storage room. While art supplies neatly lined shelves on a wall, part of the space had been cordoned off by a hanging sheet. It was the round table housed within a square frame and dominating the space that fascinated him.

"That's a casting wheel." Securing the lamp, she pulled up a stool and motioned him to sit. "I only have one smock, but you're welcome to it."

Sitting, he declined the offered garment, pulling her between his legs instead. "You use it." Fingering the straps of her dress—its warm gold a caress and complement to her midnight-rich skin—he kissed the valley between her breasts. "Preserve this pretty ball dress."

"Learn good, and I might let you peel all this pretty off. Face the wheel."

He reluctantly obeyed, thoughts hot with her carnal promise.

"Pay attention to that pedal near your feet."

"What's its purpose?"

"Try it," she gently encouraged, turning on a small battery-operated radio before retrieving a bowl of water and what, in the lamp-lit room, looked to Chase like an unformed mound of mud.

He depressed the pedal. The wheel whirred into action. He varied pressure, noting differences in speed.

"You gonna wind up with a problem on your hands, pumping hot and fast like that." Chase felt the wind of her rich laughter when she positioned herself behind him. "Stop the wheel, honey, and place this clay on it."

"Baby, I'mma humor you, but this ain't the teaching or telling I need."

He felt her soft, full breasts against his back as she reached over him, sprinkling water from the bowl onto the wheel before taking his hands and submerging them.

Her voice was a purr shooting heat to his lower region already tight with need. "Pay close attention, Chase, and I'll teach you to touch the inside of me."

He had no interest in playing clay games. He wanted all of her, wanted to travel a sensuous trail up and down her lush physique, and rest in the jeweled heaven between her legs. Only hard-learned and tightly held discipline allowed indulgence in her tortuous play.

"Chase, honey…" He sensed her suppressed snicker. "That there's a…*mess!*"

He took no offense at her assessment. The blob of clay before him looked worse than when he began.

Accepting the towel she offered, he dried his clean, freshly-scrubbed hands. "My teacher was terrible."

Ava laughed. "I reckon she is."

"Come here, woman, and show me how to do this."

"There's only one stool, so you gonna need to move."

Refusing, Chase patted his thighs. He waited, watched her consider.

"Keep your foot on that wheel, your hands to yourself, and pay attention, *Mr.* Jenkins."

She's two women in one, he decided.

Her transformation wasn't lost on him. Ava, the artist, was tranquil, quiet. Methodically, she manipulated her medium with the patience and finesse of a mother loving her child. Even so, her passion and sensuality were apparent as well as abundant.

"Place your hands on my arms…a few inches or more above my wrists." Perched on his lap—her back against his chest—her voice was authoritative yet soft and tender, forcing him to strain to hear her words above the radio's music.

"Feel that, Chase?"

"Yeah, baby, I do."

"Clay's like a woman. It's responsive. When touched right, clay moves…undulates with you. Slow the wheel a bit…"

Kissing Ava's bare arm, he did.

He noted the husky timbre of her voice when she continued. "I can cone this clay." He watched Ava dunk her hands in the bowl of water. "I can take this clay up high…and bring it back down again."

He slowly moved his wide hands up her arms, softly massaging feminine muscles that flowed and flexed as she demonstrated.

"What else you wanna do with it?" Chase whispered in her ear.

He grinned when she hesitated as if catching her breath. He lost his grin, felt himself throb with extreme need when she whispered in return,

"Make it wet."

"Why?" he husked, slowly trailing his tongue down her neck, pleased by his effect on her when she answered with concerted effort.

"Too dry...it'll crack...too wet, it'll...sop up...and cave in. Water's the..."

"Lubricant," he supplied, brushing the dress straps aside until the garment slipped downward, exposing her shoulders and back. He felt her spine curve as he stroked the silk of her skin. "Lubricant..."

"Helps movement," she barely managed. "Keeps your woman," Ava shook her head, "your *clay*...pliant."

Kissing her back, he lifted his foot from the pedal and allowed the wheel to still. "Pliant, huh?"

"Necessary during...friction...helps with...speed...and...depth...."

"Whatchu know 'bout that?" he seductively challenged, continuing his shower of kisses down Ava's spine. Fists full of her long gown, he slid the garment up her shapely legs. He delighted in her increased inhalations against him.

"Speed...depth...supply pressure. Pressure...shapes..."

"Like this?" Chase asked, drawing the gown higher, exposing Ava's strong thighs clad in silken stockings secured by garters.

His wide grip possessively palming, molding, manipulating her flesh, seconds passed with Chase and Ava immersed in the sounds of her labored breaths.

"A potter needs to know...when," she exhaled, "...where...how to touch...and how...much."

With strenuous effort, he steadied himself against the inferno unleashed by Ava's tutorial that flowed like *double entendres* housing a passion that melded with his.

"You're a damn beautiful woman, Ava Lydell," Chase rasped against a backdrop of bluesy jazz floating about the small confines. "Is my touch too much?"

A soft moan tumbled from her lips confirming that his touch was expert and absolutely enough. Hooking her arm backwards behind his neck, she was speechless.

Ava atop his lap, he widened his seated position, simultaneously

THE ART OF LOVE

widening her legs in the process. His strong hands caressed her, moving higher and higher up her thighs until encountering flimsy, frilly fabric that proved no deterrent to his intent.

Chase slid a wide hand beneath her waistband, and covered her femininity entirely. Her ensuing gasp was pure pleasure—exciting and inciting. He took his time slipping her panties from beneath her behind, down her sweet thighs until she was natural and bare. Claiming her femininity as his, Chase's fingers were gentle, insistent when uncovering and discovering Ava's warm folds. Gently, skillfully, he touched, caressed, stroked and stoked her to breathlessness.

Her hips slowly moving on his lap, in synchronization with his tantalizing touch, Chase slid his free hand up her waist, cupped a yet covered breast. "Naw, baby, leave it," he instructed when her clay-coated hands reached to free herself to him. Using her gown to his advantage, he tenderly rubbed the soft material against her engorged nipples, intent on heightening her sensations and torment.

His movements were steady, deliberate. Tortuous. For Chase, Ava's throaty purring was music.

Relentless, he used his hot tongue to brand her shoulders, her neck, her back—his mouth's ministrations enhancing the artfulness of his ceaseless hands.

"Oh...my...Lord..."

Hearing the rawness of her voice, he relinquished her breast only to lock an arm about her waist, anchoring her in place. Intentionally, he widened his thighs as much as the stool allowed, making more of her available to him. Cupping her femininity, he gently slid one finger, then another into her dampness. Coaxing, whispering his own searing desire in her ear, Chase masterfully kneaded and caressed until her gyrating body arched, and wetness coated his hand as sounds of extreme pleasure exploded from Ava's lips.

He held her, allowing her body to vibrate and tremble against his only for a moment before lifting Ava from his lap, hungry for his own carnal satiation.

He turned her to face him.

Quickly, he discarded the dress bunched about her waist, letting the gown fall at her feet as she braced his shoulders as if weak.

Hungrily, Chase gorged himself with the sight of her satin nudity made brilliant by shimmering lamplight. She was the epitome of femininity, clad solely in silken stockings and black lacy garter belt at her waist that had somehow remained intact. His blood raced with their added allure as he touched her with wonder akin to reverence, rolling down and removing her stockings so that he experienced the full effects of her softness. Her own wandering touch mirrored his as she lifted his A-shirt over his head, allowing her touch to explore his muscled hardness. When she freed him from his remaining clothing, piling them with her own garments, reverence was forgotten. Appetite dominated, instead.

Gripping her hips, he maneuvered her onto his lap, positioning her, guiding both of their movements so that she slowly took him in. A sumptuous sigh accompanied Ava's head lolling back. Chase struggled with breath.

He found bottomless pleasure in her fully encasing him, the generosity of her hips, the succulence of her breasts. Caressing one, then the other, he bathed and licked, sucked and savored as he began slowly pulsing in and out of her decadent moistness.

Moaning, Ava matched his every movement. Arms about his neck, she undulated against him, uttering delicious, nonsensical noises.

Clutching her buttocks, he meshed their mouths. Her tongue tangoed with his as their bodies increased speed, depth, friction. When she locked her legs about his back, her sweetness gripping him, her hips rotating a figure-eight around his engorgement, Chase surrendered to explosive bliss.

His detonation was fierce, the sounds of his pleasure astronomically intense.

Chase embraced Ava with every vestige of his strength, thrusting forcefully until she buried her face in his neck, her cry signaling her volatile pleasure, again.

That's when Chase felt something implode in his inner being, deeper than flesh. Breathing Ava in, it was a sensation he could only call *falling*.

CHAPTER TEN
Ava

S he sat on the floor, reclined against a wall studying the man's supreme nakedness.

That body is a work of art, Ava concluded, desperately yearning to capture Chase in paint—immortalizing every line and plane of his beauty and brilliance, nearly as much as she longed to taste him, again.

"What's your preference? Pottery or painting?"

In her lamp-lit studio, she surveyed him moving from canvas to canvas, pleased by his rapt fascination with her work.

"If you had to choose between the two, baby, which would you?"

"Don't know that I could," she admitted. "My dirt-eating Oklahoma self loves the feel of wet clay on my fingers; but, my prim and inward lady-me prefers a paintbrush."

His low chuckle rolled over her, delighting something in her that shouldn't be.

She had never shared intimacy with a man so quickly. A strict, religious upbringing had shaped the rules and guidelines of her adult living. In her unmarried state, one man was one too many. It wasn't until moving to California and fully giving in to her inward artist, that Ava allowed herself the expressive liberty of a man's physical company. While utterly enjoying the splendor, she valued her privacy as well as her intimacy and fiercely limited the men rolling in and out of her bed. Three years past thirty, Ava remained self-protective. Chase was her third man.

"This is magnificent," he murmured removing a vivid painting from her only easel.

As are you, Chase Jenkins, she silently lusted, delighting in his admiration of her artwork. She wasn't a novice to praise for her craft, but hearing it from his lips was worth savoring. The man, himself, was savor-worthy. She'd found in him a highly expressive, obviously experienced, lover whose finesse and prowess were unmatched by the men in her past. He was attentive, touching her as if she were priceless and precious—showing himself in tune with her body as well as her being. He gave liberally, delighting in her intense satisfaction time and again. But it was the tenderness with which he touched her and cosigned her right to the pleasure she experienced that had Ava feeling as if something within her was open beyond her ability to shut it again.

"That's Goodness and Mercy," she supplied as he stood enthralled by the painting of two spirit-like women in flowing blue dresses walking across a stream—reminiscent of Jesus on the sea. "It's my all-time favorite."

"Surely, goodness and mercy shall follow me all the days of my life," Chase quoted the Psalm to her delight. "When did you paint this?"

"Two years ago."

He glanced at her, amazement clouding his tone. "And it's never been purchased? When was your last exhibit?"

"The twenty-fifth of never." She laughed at herself, and his backward glance.

"You've never had an exhibit?"

Ava shrugged. "Don't know many Colored folks liable to afford any of this. Plus, the way things are right now, not too many white folks 'round here interested in sponsoring a Negro artist."

"Have you ever had a patron?"

She hesitated. Her business was hers, but in the aftermath of their lovemaking, she felt a connection and comfort with Chase that didn't come easy.

She confided her windfall blessing.

"You telling me that since I last saw you, someone paid your salon rent in full for the next six months?"

Ava nodded, amazed at God's grace and tickled by Chase's incredulous expression.

"The person's obviously an art lover," he marveled. "You should consider discussing their sponsoring an exhibit."

"I can't track anonymous." She leaned her head back against the wall with a sigh. "Lord *knows* I'm grateful for the blessing, but what comes of it remains to be seen. I might find myself sitting here painting and throwing clay for nothing. I'm still tryna get a buying audience…" Ava let her voice trail off, silencing her complaint, refusing to be an ingrate.

"Why'd you come here instead of Harlem?"

She appreciated the way Chase returned Goodness and Mercy to its easel with particular care. His reverence for her work had her divulging.

"Actually…I did stop in Harlem on my way here." Playing with the sheet wound about her, she shrugged. "It didn't work in my favor, and I heard tale that San Francisco's artsy fartsies might make room for a Colored gal and her goals."

"Are you settled here, or is anywhere else calling your name?"

Ava considered the question before shaking her head. "I'm settled. Harlem was my only other fantasy, but it's flooded to the full and even the Talented Tenth is hurting." Ava enjoyed the cool tile beneath her as she stretched her legs. "The Depression's wringing white money dry there just like it is elsewhere. Best to stay my wide behind here and work and pray 'til I get what I want. Plus, I see this paid rent as a sign from God that He wants me here. I'mma keep believing and not give up just yet."

She smiled sultrily as he approached in all his naked glory.

"Good for me."

"Good for you? Why you care where I lay my head?" she teased, accepting his helping her from her seated position on the floor. Loving the strength of his embrace, she melted against him.

"I can't have New York or nowhere else messing with my west coast loving," he threatened, hands on her behind as he slowly ground his pelvis into hers. "Ever approach Negro investors?"

Shuddering with memories of him moving deep and thick inside of her, she took her time answering. "Sweet Thing, find me some and I will." She silenced his further questioning with a kiss. Being near Chase was drug and elixir. She was addicted.

I can't get enough of you, Chase Jenkins.

Her body responding to the nearness of him, she felt off-kilter when he pulled back to ask, "You got any string?"

Her brow creased with curiosity. "In the back. Why?"

He kissed her temple. "You can wonder, but don't worry."

Laughing, Ava clutched the sheet about her, and waited as Chase disappeared to the back room only to return with her smock draped about his waist, a spool of twine…and *their* stool.

Her mind flooded with hot flashes of the lovemaking they'd managed on that surface. She licked her lower lip.

He laughed. "Hold on, baby, we go'n get to it. Come. Sit."

She complied. But Chase, removing her roses from their impromptu vase and snapping blooms from stems, had Ava jumping from her seat. "No, sir, indeed! What're you doing?"

"Woman, sit and watch me work."

"Chase, those are my roses!"

"I know. I gave them to you. Now, shhh. Please."

Casting him an evil-eye, she folded her arms across her breasts and watched the demolishment.

Her annoyance quickly dissipated, was replaced by fascination. Her smock draped about his waist was ludicrous, but the deftness of his hands proved amazing. With impressive skill, he carefully transformed her twelve cream-colored blossoms into a blooming garland.

"This was the only gift I ever saw my father make for my mother, and the only pretty thing I know how to do."

Sweetness flowed like honey through Ava's veins at Chase fastening the fragrant blossoms about her throat, creating a floral necklace. Experiencing a depth of feeling far below her surface, she murmured, "Why?"

"You gave me something priceless tonight." At her questioning look, he supplied, "You gave me your true you."

Emotions exposed, she stroked his face. Her tender touch descended to his ribcage, soothing flesh and muscle pounded by thugs the night they met. Every place Ava touched, her lips kissed.

"You could've left this off." Removing her smock from about his waist, Ava took him in hand. A guttural groan escaping his lips, he throbbed hot and rigid against her palm.

She'd barely stroked him before she found herself being lifted. Face-to-face with Chase, legs about his waist, when he backed them against the wall she was beyond ready to give him all the heat she had left.

Ava awakened amid a flurry of petals, her limbs entangled with the man in her "bed".

This old thing is worth its weight.

She wore a lazy smile, humored that the cot in the rear room behind the hanging sheet hadn't given way beneath their frenzied loving.

She inhaled, feeling languid and full of life. She had no embarrassment at the way she'd shared herself with him. She'd been untamed—unlocked and unblocked—giving more of her true self than ever given. Her face warmed, recalling wonders shared, his making *damn* good on his prior promise to taste all of her. His riding thick and deep inside, her legs clamped over his shoulders, her launch into the stratosphere. The man was immeasurably fulfilling. Purely magnetic.

Stretching, Ava tried to disentangle herself. Even in sleep, Chase's arm remained locked about her waist.

She glanced at the ceiling, hearing sounds of morning life overhead. She needed to get to the communal bathroom upstairs to handle her business, wash herself with down-home remedies that prevented conception.

"Why do you keep a cot back here?"

Presuming him asleep, Ava startled at Chase's deep baritone. Turning in his arms, she greeted him with a gentle kiss. "Morning, love."

"Morning, beautiful. I'm mighty glad for this cot, but why the need?" Chase persisted.

Feathering a finger over his brows, she didn't reiterate the evenings being her opportunity to create after days at the diner. How at times the Muse took over, leaving her crafting until the dark hours of morning; and how it was best to nap there before heading to the waitressing that waited. She dispensed with explanations that framed facts to her advantage. Rather, she offered honest truth.

"Home is here. Those boxes and suitcases over there? They're my chifforobe." She pointed out the length of string strung between two nails and the hand-washed garments draped over it to dry: her makeshift clothesline. "That hurricane lamp? It's the electricity I can't afford. And those overhead footsteps? Shop owners and 'neighbors' headed to our common commode." She kissed him again. "*Here* is where I live."

She watched him digest the information, take it all in. "That why you were hot as a hornet when we met? Being kicked out of here would've had you homeless?"

"I already was," she admitted.

Protective of Lurlene, Ava omitted her reference in telling a tale of leaving a shared space where, day and night, random men came and went.

"I came home one night. Lur…my roommate was occupied with a "visitor" and had two more sitting on the porch, waiting. One of those fools wanted to pay me to take her place."

Removed from the situation, she could laugh at something that held no humor then.

The same man returned for a full week, seeking her attention. Entering her room one evening to find the man stark naked in her bed, "relieving" himself while smelling her clothing, Ava "backslid".

"Honey, I cussed that fool sideways from here to Hades and back again." The subsequent war of words between her and Lurlene had been vicious. Her sanctuary violated, she'd felt betrayed. Lurlene had damaged their trust by attempting to draw Ava in, by intentionally imposing on her, her own choice to "entertain" men for money. Ava left that same night, refusing to spend another minute in mess and madness. Unable to afford even a room in a boardinghouse, Ava made use of the diner's storage room knowing the secret of her homelessness was—unlike her studio where Mr. Randolph often dropped in for "random spot checks"—safe there.

Loving Lurlene like a God-sent sister, the two eventually made amends. In hindsight, she admitted she should've left when Lurlene first chose to turn their abode into a harlot's den.

"Why didn't you?"

Stroking Chase's chest, her voice held no rancor when answering, "Same reason you chose rum-running. Limitations…and convenience." The hurtful truth she chose to eliminate was that when times were bleakest, penniless and perilous, she'd been forced to fight off the temptation to participate.

Ava watched Chase chew his words a while, deciding which to speak and which to swallow. "The woman you were with last night at Brown's? Is she the roommate?"

"There's no need for that knowledge." She interrupted his objection. "You hold your secrets, sweet baby. I'll hold mine."

"What secrets do you think I have, Ava?"

She smiled at his irritated tone. "Whether or not you're still rum-running, and what those fools were really after. 'Cause, honey, I was born at night, but not yesterday. They were after much more than money."

She studied him, saw his face change from vexed to dangerous.

"What makes you think I'm not the one pursuing them?"

Ava slid a leg between his. "I guess that's inevitable on account of your name," she playfully stated. "What're you chasing today?"

Again, she observed his emotions switch and change. His thick, luscious lips lifted into a hungry grin. "Some deep, dark chocolate."

She shuddered when Chase cupped her breast and lowered his head to worship it, his beard an additional torment that tickled her skin. When he repositioned her onto her back, she relinquished any and all thoughts of unpleasantness. Greedily, she submitted to his loving, her need to bathe with preventative remedies forgotten and forsaken.

CHAPTER ELEVEN
Chase

O ver and again, he rolled a coin from finger to finger, bombarded by the thought that Domino Garamelli somehow knew his business.

Domino's popping up in northern California reaffirmed it, and his youngest brother's death provided painful evidence: there was a break in the Jenkins chain. A leak and a snitch existed in their midst.

Chase preferred to leave Garamelli and every evil he represented in Los Angeles. The bastard gave bootleggers a bad name—hijacking shipments, informing on the competition, breaking into warehouses and thieving others' supplies. Garamelli was greedy...and sloppy. Evidence of his presence was always left behind. But because of his Mafia connections, few bothered to respond to Domino's double-handed corruption. Chase had. Sylas was dead because of it.

"You looking kinda winded, Jenkins. Did she sap your strength?"

He swallowed grief as hard as he could while eyeing the man entering the room smiling like he knew something. "'Bout as much as she took you."

Kissing his bandaged arm, Ray Poundsey seated himself opposite Chase, grudgingly laughing. "Best mind your manners and not cross that one there. That woman cuts like an overseer's whip."

Leaning back in his chair, Chase quietly chuckled at his childhood friend's assessment.

A whip she is, he silently concurred, resisting the temptation to ruminate on Ava or the mind-shattering depths of her good loving. He needed to be fully present, and clear thinking. "I owe you and that cut-up arm."

"Yeah, you do!" Poundsey agreed, a scowl descending. "You still haven't explained why you weren't where we agreed to be and when."

Chase's eyes were like flint, reflecting his inner disgust at having lost an opportunity to blindside Garamelli, of striking a cobra strategically. Being chivalrous and helping Ava with her delivery had proven costly and near deadly.

Chivalrous nothing! You wanted that woman.

"I was sidetracked," he admitted, loathing his own failure, while wrestling a willingness to kill.

Rolling the coin between his thumb and forefinger, Chase's vision swam with images of his mother bent over her son's coffin wailing as if the human embodiment of pain and brokenness. Whatever his faults, he honored life too much to take one. But, blood required blood.

He believed in family honor, and handling responsibilities despite degree of difficulty. He was prepared to do whatever was needed. Yet, the intuitiveness in him questioned the providence behind his failure. Had Ava been a divine intervention and godsend? Heaven's way of keeping Chase from homicidal bedlam?

He might be a murderer if his woman hadn't turned his head. His focus and discipline in business was always executed with precision. Pleasure *never* preceded it. Until Ava Lydell. "Who's feeding Garamelli?"

Poundsey's mustached mouth turned down with distaste at his inability to put missing pieces into place. "I'm still digging, Rum Money."

"Only dig deep enough. Keep yourself safe," Chase instructed, uneasy at the thought of another beloved being in harm's way. He and Poundsey went too far back for Chase to put Poundsey's life on the line.

Friends since boys in knee breeches, Poundsey had come into the business only after Sylas' death. His loyalty saw Poundsey positioning himself as an insider, as one of Garamelli's men. Both knew the dangers and the risks. Chase couldn't allow error-making, yet he had. He'd failed to meet Poundsey in the Oakland Hills when Garamelli's entourage consisted of only one other man. Because of lusting for Ava.

Her art delivery occurring at the basin of the Hills, placed him in close proximity. Close wasn't enough, and Chase had forfeited his chance. Instead, Garamelli found him.

Stretching long, well-muscled legs, Chase considered the small, but tidy room about him. Commandeering the entire top floor of Mz. Delsie's boardinghouse had afforded him necessary privacy in which to transact business. In this very room, Poundsey had, days ago, delivered needed information on Garamelli's movements.

Poundsey's insight proving true, Garamelli had left the Oakland Hills at the indicated time. Unfortunately for Chase, while aiding Ava, his own position hadn't been prime. Instead, traveling downhill in route to the San Francisco peninsula where a rum delivery waited, Garamelli had somehow encountered Chase. He'd unwittingly served himself on a platter to his enemy; and Domino Garamelli struck first, causing their collision and confrontation. What he hoped would be an advantage became the enemy's win.

Named for his mother, Sylla's Delivery Service was the signage on the side of his truck. It was legitimate, innocuous, and didn't lead back to rum running or even Chase. How, then, did Garamelli know that particular truck was his to target and attack?

His vexation over the violent encounter was mollified only by the fact that Garamelli had missed out on a rum shipment. Ava handling that pistol and popping tires saw to that.

"Whatchu smiling about, Jenkins?"

"Mind your business."

The boyhood friends, now men, considered each other knowingly. Seconds later, they were both chuckling.

"Mmm-hmm, Rum Money. Told you last night that hot choco-late woman had you!"

"That, you did." *And that she does!* Chase inwardly admitted, reaching for the beer he'd long ignored. It was flat, warm, and taste-less.

"So…whatchu plan to do about her? She alright with you making messy money by running rum?"

"That woman's lips can sanctify my bankbook with one kiss."

Poundsey laughed soundly. "Maybe, but you still ain't never planted roots over a woman. You keep things moving. Plus, you're only here, up north, for a quick minute at the most."

Chase sat a moment before bowing his head and kneading the bridge of his nose. How to undo the fact that this Bay Area reloca-tion was a temporary ruse to draw out the man he suspected was his brother's killer?

He'd left Los Angeles thanks to the breach in his operation that made remaining there unsafe for anyone remotely connected to him. His relocation was double-fold: to protect those he loved, and to lure Domino Garamelli beyond his own safety zone. Once the mission was accomplished, his intent was to return home. Now, there was

Ava.

"I'll work it out," he vowed aloud. Would Ava come to the southern part of the state with him…once the unpleasantness of bad blood was finished, and life was clear? Whatever the outcome, in the meantime, he needed to make sure she was safe. "I'm pulling you off Garamelli."

"What the hell for?"

"You got inside and got what info you could. That was our goal. We're good." Leaning forward, Chase placed the gold coin found near his brother's dead body atop the table. "I want you on Ava. When I'm not with her, you are."

"Why? Garamelli ain't even mentioned her."

"Not yet."

He watched Poundsey take his words in. "You concerned he might try to get to you by finding out who she is and harming her somehow?"

Eyes reflecting a stormy darkness, Chase replied, "He'll wake up playing dice with the devil if he does."

Poundsey grinned. "So…she ain't no temporary taste then?"

Staring at the gold coin on the table, Chase shook his head. He intended to have Ava. Today. Tomorrow. For always.

"Uncle C.J.!"

The door being thrown open, and a child racing in, prevented Chase answering. Hazel-eyed and sandy-haired, he was swift on five-year-old legs.

Chase had barely pushed away from the table, before the child threw himself into his uncle's lap. "Little Sy!"

"Uncle C.J., I helped Uncle Marlon with the money!" the child proudly sang.

"What money?" Chase asked, hugging his nephew—the living proof his dead brother, Sylas, ever existed. His brother's only child was stamped with his father's appearance and temperament, as if Sylas had bargained with heaven to leave a portion of himself to live again.

"The money for the store man, and I didn't drop any of it."

Glancing at Poundsey, Chase's jaw was instantly rigid.

His middle brother, Marlon, had involved their nephew in grown men's business? He knew Marlon's predisposition for the flagrant, but this was flat out ignorant. "Where's Uncle Marlon?"

"Right here."

Chase looked up to find his middle brother, leaned against the doorjamb, too indolent to enter. Only the fact that a child was present kept him from stalking over and locking a massive grip about Marlon's neck.

Gottdamn fool!

"Did I do good, Uncle C.J.?"

Extracting a quarter from his pants pocket, Chase grinned, tickled by his nephew's eyes increasing in size and delight. "You did just fine. Here, you earned it. Don't spend it all at one time."

"I won't, 'cause Daddy said a real man oughta keep something to warm his hands. I'mma real man just like him, right?"

"You're well on your way, Little Sy." Chase mussed the blond curls on his nephew's head before lifting the child from his lap. "Do me a favor? Go downstairs and see if Mz. Delsie might need help with anything. I'll take you out and let you spend some of your riches in a minute."

He waited as his nephew scampered happily away before redirecting his attention to his middle brother, whom Chase hated to admit, was becoming increasingly useless.

Too much like the old man, he decided. Marlon resembled their father most, looking as if their mother's Negro blood hadn't danced with their father's Creole. Of their parents' five children, Marlon and Sylas had inherited their father's fair pigment; whereas, Chase and his older sisters blended Papa's pale with their mother's rich, sable brown skin. While Sylas had used paleness to advance their business; Marlon used his selfishly. Marlon played with the color line, running with white women.

"You can stop shooting me in your mind, C.J., everything worked the way you wanted."

Though not the oldest child, Chase was the firstborn son, and had been groomed to fend for his siblings. He had always taken that responsibility serious in his useless father's absence. Eyeing his middle brother lounging in the doorway as if the world was his to give, he felt like snatching the belt from his slacks and reminding Marlon who was older.

"Take that child on another run and you'll be digging my foot out your ass for weeks. Clear?"

Marlon's nonchalant shrug was his answer.

"I asked, are we clear?"

"Yeah…sure, Chase, crystalline. Why you renting a storefront anyhow? You setting up new business?"

Chase ignored the question. "Why'd you bring Little Sylas to the Bay Area to begin with?"

"You asked me that already!"

"Obviously, the answer wasn't sufficient."

"I owed him a train ride…and he missed you."

While different physically, Chase and Sylas were nearly twins in personality and disposition. Little Sylas seemed to cling to Chase since his father's death. Yet, he didn't swallow Marlon's logic that he'd brought their nephew to see him solely for Little Sylas' benefit. His brother was obviously involved in something, perhaps, less than salient.

"I want you and Little Sy on a train heading home by the weekend."

"Say what?" Marlon snorted. "Whose daddy are you? You don't get to—"

Chase interrupted, his voice low and even. "I spoke once. That's enough. I won't say it again."

He could practically view the angry waves rolling off of Marlon. Though older than Sylas, Marlon was a hot-head who'd been bested in business by their youngest brother. Still, Marlon had better sense than to test Chase. Tossing a sullen glance Poundsey's way, Marlon left.

Chase swore beneath his breath. Marlon's behavior had proven more and more problematic since Sylas' death. He understood the grief. At times, his own felt monumental. But there was something more in Marlon…a brewing undercurrent that felt questionable and elusive.

"You want me to make sure he boards that train like you asked?"

Leaning back in his chair, Chase folded strong arms behind his head and studied the ceiling a moment. "No…he knows I'm not playing."

"So, how am I getting off Garamelli's squad?"

"I'mma have you arrested."

"*Hell, naw*, Negro, you full of nonsense!"

Chase chuckled softly. "Relax yourself, Ray. It's nothing more than a set-up to get you out without raising suspicion. The cop's an actor and associate. It won't be real." He looked at his closest, lifelong friend. "Trust me on it?"

Ray Poundsey sucked his teeth indignantly. "Man, I don't have a choice but to. Still don't know why I stick with your ugly ass!"

"'Cause my ugly makes yours look good."

The men shared a laugh.

"So says that sweet peach I met last night at the Ballroom."

"Negro, you still fabricating make-believe women?" Chase taunted.

"This one's *real* real. In fact, she's the one was at the table with your Mighty Ms. Ava."

"Can't say I noticed her much if at all," Chase admitted, sitting up and considering his friend.

"Man, that woman got you *that* whipped?" Poundsey shook his head. "Good for her. 'Bout time some woman did." Poundsey glanced at his watch. "Speaking of Lurlene—that's sweet peach's name—I need to clean myself up. I'm taking her to dinner." Poundsey pushed away from the table. "You and Ava wanna join us? They obviously know each other."

Looking out the window, Chase noted the April breeze swirling, dancing through the leaves. The sun was muted, content with the loving touch of a cool spring. Even from indoors, the springtime Bay Area air appeared chilly.

He stood with Poundsey. "Thanks, but no. Ava doesn't need to know we're connected just yet. Plus, I got better plans."

"Such as?"

"Getting some hot chocolate to warm my mouth and my hands."

CHAPTER TWELVE
Ava

Ava sat pleased and amazed by the outcome of Chase's suggestion. His relocating her pottery wheel to the front of her studio, suggesting she raise the door and window shades as a way of sharing her artistic process and inviting the outside in proved genius.

I shoulda thought of this!

She was true artist, protectively sequestering her products until completion. This opening the window to her world—as well as propping her *Art by Ava* sign outside against the building—had invited more than one passerby in, allowing her to engage in conversation about her passion.

Despite a morning shift at the diner, Ava was energized, nearly high. Just before opening the studio, she'd treated herself to a rare bubble bath to soak away a night of Chase-induced exhaustion. She hadn't made one sale, but the increased interest and curiosity of others was infectious.

"Mama, may I try?"

"No, just hush and watch!"

Finishing a stroke, Ava lifted her paintbrush, leaving it aloft like a maestro's baton. Forcing her focus from her painting of a mason jar brimming with gladiolas, she smiled at the child clutching her mother's hand, brown eyes wide with wonder.

"This picture is missing something," Ava mused.

"What?" the little girl asked, only to be shushed again.

Ava offered the mother a smile, beckoned the child. "Come help me figure it out." Chewing the end of her paintbrush, she feigned confusion. "What do you think?" Life as the firstborn of eighteen had taught her tolerance.

Standing beside her, the child was suddenly shy. "It's pretty."

"Thanks, sweetie, but don't you think it could use a little something special? What's your favorite color?"

"Pink."

Ava snapped her fingers. "*Pink?* That's precisely what this painting needs." Dabbing brush in paint, she extended it towards the girl, whose head immediately swiveled towards her mother seeking permission.

"Ma'am, you don't have to—"

Placing the brush in the little girl's hand, Ava waved the objection away. The joy spreading like sunrise over the child's face was worth any alterations as she gently guided, coaxed and instructed. "Now, that there's a masterpiece!" Removing the nine-by-twelve canvas from its rickety easel, Ava handed it to her protégé. "Here, honey, take this home and show everybody what you did."

It took a moment to talk the mother into accepting the gift, which segued into a conversation about the child's always being in trouble for 'coloring with Crayolas and scribbling on things' on which she had no business drawing. The child's fascination and the mother's lament left Ava proposing something she'd never considered: art lessons. Bubbling with excitement, she made the proposition.

"But we're simple folks, and all this is so fancy!" The mother indicated the studio. "Plus...we don't have much."

"Honey, who does?" Ava gently questioned, determined to overturn—at least in this child's life—the lies told, that art was for the rich and white. She stubbornly assured the woman they'd negotiate an agreeable fee, even if it meant bartering.

Seeing the family out, she stood on the sidewalk a moment, thrilled by a new prospect, thankful she had something to offer others.

Returning indoors, Ava made quick work of tidying up her surroundings. Task complete, she found herself in front of Goodness and Mercy, recalling Chase's astonishment that it hadn't been sold.

You've never had an exhibit?

Stroking the canvas, Ava sighed, admitting she hadn't, but her work had.

Her leaving Harlem hadn't been solely due to an inability to break through a saturated market. Rather, callousness and colorism helped her hightail it west.

Even now, her face warmed with shame and anger. But at the time she'd done what was necessary to keep bread in her mouth, a roof over her head, and live.

You simply do the work. We'll promote the event and pay you forty cents on every dollar for each piece sold.

Provided she kept her identity concealed.

When she questioned why she, the rightful artist, was unable to attend the exhibits showcasing her own art, the response Ava received was soul-searing, debilitating.

You're too dark.

White patrons wouldn't possibly believe such exquisite creations could come from a "southern talking" woman of "sooty complexion". And even if they did, patrons' comfort level was paramount to success. Sales could be hampered with their being forced to converse with someone of such "unlearned backwardness"; or worse, her "niggardliness" would be played up, making her a comical phenomenon. Such spectacle should be avoided at all cost. Thus, a suitable Colored woman of desirable skin tone was found to pose as Ava Lydell. Ava's consolation was being allowed to be present at the soiree, only while donning a maid's uniform, a food tray in hand.

Cloaked in the garb of servility, she became a mere tool for white folks' feasting. Dressed in invisibility, she was a nonentity ignored throughout the night of her first and only exhibit until being boldly, blatantly propositioned by a white man who'd imbibed three drinks too many. She'd given the groping offender a curse-laden piece of her mind before leaving, outraged and demoralized.

Mishap and indignities aside, the night proved successful with the sale of several art pieces. Her earnings, however, were reduced by claims of "unprofessionalism"—claims which would willingly be dropped if her assailant's scandalous advances were accepted on his terms.

Taking her reduced earnings, she hopped a westbound train the next night, vowing her art and her soul would never be so detestably sold again. Her paintings bore *her* signature; the deep brown of her face was the face of *this* artist. Hyper-sensitive colorists be damned.

"And to think those fool promoters were Colored as me." She shook her head and exhaled, ridding herself of old foolishness. She gladly abandoned painful memories of the past when, her back to the door, she felt the atmosphere change and shift. It was suddenly warm and thick.

"Hey, handsome," she called without turning. He was instantly behind her, inviting Ava to rest her world and lean back into his strength. She shivered when Chase kissed her neck.

"You knew it was me without looking. How?"

Ava laughed wantonly. "Let's just say I got to tingling in certain places and parts."

"Which in particular?"

Ava grabbed his wandering hands. Turning in his arms, she looked up at him. "Don't even touch me 'til I deal with you, Chase Jenkins." Pulling money from her smock, she'd stuffed it in the bib pocket of his overalls. "Keep your money, and don't make me a fool."

Ava had awakened to an empty cot, and seventy-five dollars atop the crate that served as a "bedside" table. Her initial ire had reduced to a sticky molasses of feelings that were still sore.

If you can't do for yourself, it don't get done.

Teaching she'd heard all her life ricocheted about her mind. She'd been raised poor, but proud. As the oldest child from a brood of many, she'd been conditioned to give and give again. Not receive. A man's doing for her preempted a loss of questionable control, signified her failure. Ava refused to relinquish hard-won autonomy.

"Honoring my word and repaying the money taken from you on my account makes a fool of you how?"

She suppressed a smile at his tight tone. "You're more than man enough to understand leaving money after loving a woman feels a little like you paying for something. Chase, honey, I'm not a harlot."

She watched the light change and play in his eyes. "You have permission to shoot me the day I treat you as such."

Laughing, Ava slipped from his embrace, and took her time closing the studio for the night. "Long's we're clear." She glanced over her shoulder at the sound of a humorless chuckle escaping his lips. "Is there a problem, Mr. Jenkins?"

She watched him cop a seat on *their* stool. "Just days ago you were begging me to help you deliver an art piece. Now, you're rejecting this, which is nothing more than a fulfilled debt, and looking on it like an insult on account of you're too proud to accept help from a man."

She smiled. "I won't argue that. I begged like a baby for your help when I was desperate for it. But, tonight I'm not."

"So in the course of this day everything in your life was made right?"

Ava shook her head. "No, and as long as I'm a Colored woman in this world, perfect ain't possible. That doesn't mean I don't know how to live without being bought."

"Baby, I told you when we met I don't buy female favors. Never have. Never will. So, you object to my satisfying a debt?"

"No, I object to the seedy way it was done."

Chase ran a hand over his face before holding his hands up in surrender. "Fine, baby. My granddad taught me not to argue with a woman if I wanted to win."

She laughed briefly. "What you tryna win?"

"I'll let you know when I win it. As for now, my apologies for being insulting. That wasn't my intention."

"What are you intentions, Chase Jenkins? Or do you have any?" she asked, crossing arms over breasts and leaning against the front window.

"Would you believe me if I told you?"

"Try me and see." Ava watched him approach with panther-like intensity. "Uhn-uhn, just talk, don't touch," she warned when he neared.

His resulting grin was brief-lived. "My intention is owning all of Ava Lydell."

"So…you didn't hear a thing I just said?"

"I'm talking about here, woman," Chase elaborated, touching the place over her heart. "The richest thing I want from Ava *is* Ava."

Her smile was soft, yet brilliant. "Good, 'cause Ava's the only thing I have to give. And if you want her, you best treat her right and act correct. Don't try to take care of me, Chase. I'm a hardworking Colored woman, striving, and valuing my independence. I'll let you know if and when your help is needed."

"Duly noted, even though you're wrong as five left feet. Now… may I touch you, stubborn mule?"

"After I get my money," she purred, reclaiming the bills she stuffed into the pocket. She silenced his roaring laughter with a ready kiss that effortlessly expanded into something hot and decadent. She didn't object when Chase slid the smock from her body, removed her blouse and brassiere—setting free her loveliness. She stood wanting and waiting when he did nothing, save feast visually.

Deliberately withholding his touch, Chase grinned wickedly. Blowing against her skin a steady stream of warmth, he traveled a slow path from her ear, down her neck, shoulder blades, until reaching her breasts—gently nipping before retracing his trek upward, blowing sultrily against Ava's skin. Intentionally allowing is beard to rub against her breasts, he repeated his slow blowing torment.

Ava was breathing raggedly when Chase whispered, "You need my help yet?"

Nodding, she moaned her consent.

He removed her panties, reclined her across the studio's only table. "I can never own you. That can't keep me from wanting you solely for myself. This here is how and what I win…and I'mma take my time winning it, baby, like a greedy man."

Skirt hiked about her waist, her legs over his shoulders, when Chase bent to taste, Ava was made to believe every word he said.

Brown's Ballroom proved ideal. Tonight, there was neither seeking, nor searching. She was where she wanted to be, slow dancing in the strong arms of her man.

Ava considered resistance a misuse of strength. She accepted Chase as hers because she wanted him. He could woo her to his heart's content, but she was already his. The swiftness of their love affair left her feeling undeniably beautiful, bold, and decadently brazen.

"You're wearing a loaded smile."

Snared by the soft warmth of his eyes, Ava asked, "You like it?"

"Depends on what it's loaded with."

"A fine, butterscotch man and his honey-help-me loving." Her body still tingled as if greedily hoarding the after effects of deep indulgence. Ava was too grown to be embarrassed, still she was amazed by the intimate places she'd allowed Chase to take her, places she had never been.

She felt herself further opening when he leaned down, whispering in her ear, "Baby, you're the only woman I've ever wanted to love that way. You taste better than new money."

She rippled with remembrance. "We need to talk about something else 'fore we have a pure-D problem out here."

She loved his husky laugh.

"Yeah, let's. Finish telling me how you came to art."

"Art came to me," Ava corrected. She was the little brown girl who'd visited her studio that afternoon. Always drawing, doodling. Feeling as if color lived and breathed deep in her being. "He probably wishes he never had, but my daddy made me my first paintbrush when I asked for one." She laughed. "It was an ugly mess, but Mama made me some "paint" by mashing berries and I used it."

Her laughter was girlish, recounting the origins of her love of painting, and her first piece of pottery: Oklahoma mud she shaped into a pig and baked in the oven. "My mama still has that butt-ugly thing."

"You know your body warms when you're speaking on your passion?"

She stared at him a moment before answering. "Perhaps...or that heat might have much to do with dancing in the arms of a certain man. Or maybe I'm just hot-to-trot."

"Baby, trot hot all you want as long as it's only for me," he warned, sobering suddenly. "I don't understand why you haven't been swept up by some man."

She gently traced his jaw, loving the bristly feeling of his beard beneath her fingertips, not caring that she was an old maid in the estimation of some. "Oh, I've been proposed to. Twice. I turned that foolishness down both times."

"Because?"

"The first one didn't want *me*. He wanted a piece of skirt too dumb to do anything 'cept his bidding. The second told me I could 'play with my paint' until our wedding day. After that? All that 'waste of time' was unwelcome, and the only thing he expected of me was having so many babies that I couldn't breathe."

Chase grunted. "Their being two fools before God kept you free for me."

She laughed as he twirled her in a slow pirouette that Ava suddenly stopped. A familiar figure lingering on the far side of the dance floor came into focus.

Lurlene?

"Something wrong?"

"No...just thought I saw someone," Ava answered, looking again only to find Lurlene had been joined by a man assisting her into her coat as if favoring his right arm.

Her heartbeat pounded, sensing something familiar about him.

Grabbing Chase's hand, she headed off the dance floor, moving as fast as the crowd allowed.

Maneuvering the crowd wasn't easy. By the time she reached the place Lurlene had been, Brown's Ballroom was absent of her friend.

"Ava? Everything okay?"

"I'm good, baby." She responded distractedly, thinking Lurlene shrewd and well able to protect herself. She told herself concern was misplaced…despite the man Lurlene left with appearing too similar to the man Ava cut the night she met Chase.

They both knew her protests were pitiful.

"I don't wanna be in some other woman's house with you."

Chase kissed and licked her concerns away. She held on to flimsy complaint.

"It's not right, Chase, me being in Mz. Delsie's house like this."

"Shhh, sweetheart," he soothed, reiterating his "renting" the entire top floor as if, to Ava, that made a difference. "Mz. Delsie's two floors down and sleeps like a brick."

"Don't mean it don't feel indecent."

"Yeah… real *good* and indecent," he laughingly agreed, nuzzling her neck. "Come on, baby, relax. I wanna make love to you somewhere other than on that stool or a cot." He breathed down her body. "We need to spread it wide right here on this soft bed."

Wriggling from underneath his weight, she pushed him onto his back and stared down at him. What, in this man, coaxed her to give her whole self again and again? Ava couldn't explain it. He touched her soul; she touched his. Her fingers trailing his flesh, she knew he was physically beautiful, and so much more, as if the most glorious colors in the world rested within him. He was her art of love—a masterpiece unveiling.

Ava kissed Chase, her lips like tender fire that consumed and blazed.

I might be headed to hell for acting a harlot in another woman's house, but I'm going happy.

When he gripped her hips and positioned her above so that she straddled him, Ava opened herself and fully took him in, working her feminine skills until annihilating Chase with the loving a grown woman gives.

Ensuing days and nights flowed like water and waves. Limited in income, Ava's life bloomed in other wonderful ways. She had a potential art pupil, a little protégé. The attention and affection of a man whose passion and need for her amplified daily. Her heart reciprocated, sinking her into something soft as love. Even so, she maintained a necessary resistance.

"Send it back, Chase Jenkins," was her response to every gift he gave. The new easel. The smocks. Art supplies and sundries. She refused each, unwilling to accept the largess of rum-running. While Chase neither affirmed nor denied, she suspected his involvement in bootlegging remained. Unless Sylla's Delivery Service was serving the entire Bay Area, she doubted the business afforded Chase his kind of spending. "The only thing I want from you, baby, is what you're giving: your time...and cream-colored roses."

Without fail, she received both in abundance. The diner. Her studio. Pale roses arrived—single or bouquet—until her world swam with intoxicating beauty and fragrance. Inspired, Ava painted gorgeous, life-like renditions of them.

The time he gave was just as delicious. They dined. Danced. Made love over and again, giving and getting all they could as if tomorrow wasn't promised. They visited the de Young Museum, and strolled Golden Gate Park. Ventured like sightseers on trolley cars, and cruised the bay. He even talked her into riding the elevator to the top floor of San Francisco's tallest skyscraper.

"I'll never let you get me on an elevator again!" Hours after the fact, she still reeled with the uncomfortable sensation of soaring, and falling. Walking the sidewalk, she clutched his arm for stability.

"I thought you were about to see Jesus." Chase chuckled at her expense. "You were digging your nails in me worse than when the loving's good and I got you going."

She tossed her head back and laughed. "You should hush with all that!"

"You denying it?"

"No, sir, but I'mma need to feed you a dose of humility." Ava glanced up at him, ready for his comeback. Instead, she found a look that stopped her in her tracks.

She followed his focus to where broken glass lay like fallen stars gracing the pavement. The front windows of her studio were no more. Every pane had been completely shattered.

Ava hurried ahead, only for Chase to halt her progress.

"Wait. Right. Here."

His uncompromising tone was enough for even Ava. Seeing him extract his concealed firearm left her unsettled and cognizant that she still knew too little about the one man she loved…

Her head swam with dizziness—at the notion of loving Chase, and this unmitigated mess.

Nightfall had erased foot traffic. The roadway was clear of most cars. The night silence weighed in on Ava as she waited until she couldn't tolerate another second.

Gingerly stepping over glass shards and fragments, she made her way inside her studio.

Her heart lurched with unfathomable pain at what she saw.

Shattered pottery, paintings ripped and gutted greeted her. The spirit of her art wailed in abject misery.

She covered her face to stifle the cry rolling up from her soul. The jewels of her heart, Ava's art, lay wholly desecrated and destroyed.

CHAPTER THIRTEEN
Chase

He had eaten enough anger to starve himself of good. Now, he was finished. With the rage that ripped through him at obvious vandalism, at the certainty that Domino Garamelli was involved. He had to be strategic in handling the situation. Rage would only ruin him.

Shifting in his chair, he changed his posture from reclined to upright. Fingers steepled beneath his chin, he sat and watched Ava, soothed by the soft sounds of her sleep, the rhythmic rise and fall of her chest. If a regret persisted, it was that she'd suffered another loss because of him. Being the cause of pain to the woman he loved was beyond abhorrent.

I'm damn-done-in-love with you, Ava Lydell.

He felt himself fall the moment she first spit fire in his face. Indignant and accusatory over the presumed cost of his aid. Indulging in her intimacy had merely plunged him deeper in what he meant to avoid. Denying what he felt for her was a fool's game that Chase chose not to play. He was soul-deep in love. Plain and simple. It was a liberating notion that left him smiling. Rubbing a hand through his beard, he felt his humor fade.

He had moves to make. Like convincing Ava that she could have better than living in the back of a white man's storefront as if some unwanted waif. Like gently planting the idea of her relocating to southern California…and combining her life with his in matrimony that was God-ordained.

Stubborn woman won't make it easy.

His work was truly cut out for him.

Chase stood and stretched the kinks from his frame. He inhaled a cleansing breath, his gaze landing on the one object to miraculously escape violence and vandalism: Ava's Goodness and Mercy painting.

Removing his clothing, Chase climbed into bed behind her, praying heaven's twin angels would surely follow as well as proceed them.

Turning off the bedside lamp, he lay back, sighing against the cool night. Ava's turning towards him in her sleep was welcomed warmth. He wrapped her in his arms, grateful Mz. Delsie's tea had produced a much-needed calming effect. Ava's devastation at the loss of her art was something Chase never wanted to witness again.

Tenderly, he kissed her forehead, vowing to right every wrong.

Of their own accord, his hands tenderly rubbed her back, her body, soothing her slumbering form. Her smooth skin was inviting, as was her curvaceous beauty cradled against him. Chase suppressed a too ready and rising want. Rather, he indulged in the wonders of their togetherness, as if *they* had always been. Holding her closely, he gave her the security of his embrace. He willed her peace and well-being, his heart wide with the varying facets of love a man could and should give.

The clean-up crew he assembled had swiftly righted the mess vandals made. While Ava's art was unsalvageable, the studio was easily restored, and broken windows boarded over until the glass could be replaced. Seeing that what could be well was, Chase proceeded with his day's deliveries.

He worked diligently. He preferred mind and body remain busy. He brought the same detail and care to Sylla's Delivery Service as he had rum-running. While Sylas had been the front man, charming customers with his white smile and Creole infectiousness, Chase was the steady, the strategist, and mind-power that afforded their operation successes not common to Colored bootleggers. Chase brought that acumen to Sylla's.

Sylla's was his walk-away from the old life, and entry into the legitimate. It was a set-up that would never garner but a fraction of the vast income he made bootlegging, but Chase had wisely invested. If his affairs remained properly handled, he was financially set for years if not for life.

I'm still hustling and delivering, just legally this time, he mused, parking his truck in front of Mz. Delsie's. Neighborhood children had obviously enjoyed playtime activities in the long driveway. Walking up the drive, Chase pushed aside the homemade, handmade "toys" left behind.

He was tired. The day had been long with new customers added to the route. He wanted a bath, a meal, and Ava.

Entering the backdoor, he was humored by the sight greeting

him.

She was in the kitchen cooking, singing, hips swinging in sync to music drifting from the parlor's phonograph. He easily stole up behind her, pressing his body to hers.

"You 'bout to burn it down with all this rump-rolling," he warned, gripping her hips and moving with the music.

Her laughter was lyrical. "Nothing's burning in this kitchen 'cept you." Ava turned to face him. "Now move yourself somewhere before Mz. Delsie comes back."

"Where is she?"

She looked towards the ceiling. "Fixing up a room for a new boarder."

"How's she treating you?"

Mz. Delsie—Chase's godmother and his mother's dearest friend—was fundamentally kind, but didn't take to "random women" beneath her roof. The boardinghouse had strict rules that he had obviously violated.

"The woman's a godsend, Chase. Now move!"

His lips lifted salaciously. "Fast? Slow? Deep? Just a tease? How you want me moving, Miss Lady?"

"Away from me."

Chuckling, Chase stole a kiss before peeking over her shoulders at the pot of greens on the stove. "Can you cook?"

"Did those sweet potato pies lie?"

"No ma'am, but baking ain't cooking, and cooking ain't baking."

"Bye, Chase, go take a bath so I can earn my keep."

"There's nothing for you to earn, baby. You're my guest."

Her growing quiet and moving beyond his reach weren't lost on him. He studied her stiff posture a moment before asking, "What's going on, Ava?"

Ladling greens into a serving dish, she spoke quietly. "That room Mz. Delsie's readying is for me. She refuses to accept my money, and I refuse charity." Ava lifted the greens. "Least I can do is cook long's I'm here."

Her moving into the dining room afforded him a needed moment. Ava Lydell was enough to make a man scream.

He had been hard-pressed to earn her agreement that remaining at her storefront studio wasn't safe. When her emotions abated, she acquiesced to his request that she lodge with him, removed from harm's way. Obviously, Ava had decided that doing so was morally distasteful.

He remained silent as she came in and out of the kitchen, carting dinner to the dining room table. When she'd finished and removed her apron, Ava gave him her attention.

"When I finished my shift at the diner, I went by the studio. I thank you with all my heart for doing what you did to set it in order again. And bless you for giving me a place to lay my head."

He was motionless as she stood before him, laying a gentle hand against his chest.

"But I won't disrespect this woman's house by using it to lay up with you. My staying here means I have my own room."

Stiff-lipped, Chase accepted, without reciprocating, Ava's kiss. Turning, he left Ava to her business, withholding the fact that the house they lodged in was, in fact, owned by him.

Night was velvet in its embrace about him. His breathing was shallow, his thoughts like wispy fog trailing the middle floor to Ava.

She'd gone to bed, in *her* room, without him. Made sure he understood the door would be locked and bolted.

Damn woman's two shades short of sane, he decided, on the verge of fitful slumber. Before he could drift fully into the arms of sleep, his hearing honed in on the sound of footsteps pounding. Instinctively, Chase reached for his firearm and quickly slipped on his pants.

By the time he reached the hall, Poundsey was already there, breathless from three flights of stairs. "I told you put a damn phone in your room!"

"Why? What's going on?" Chase slipped his gun beneath the back of his waistband.

"Ms. Sylla!" Poundsey panted.

Chase felt suddenly cold. His voice was low and dangerous. "What's wrong with my mother?"

"She's fine. It's Little Sy. He just got home."

He stared at Poundsey as if the man was missing his mouth. His brother Marlon had returned to southern California with Little Sylas two days ago.

Everything in him did a slow melt listening to Poundsey convey Sylas's being taken to a Los Angeles police precinct by the Pullman porter who found the child aboard the Colored train car, alone and fast asleep.

The good Lord be praised, his nephew was home where he belonged, and safe.

"Marlon?" Chase pointlessly asked.

Poundsey shook his head. "In the wind."

Chase punched the wall before leaning against it.

"Man…I been holding my tongue and ain't said nothing…but we gotta face facts. Your brother's the break in our chain."

His face was a mask of angry angles when returning Poundsey's point-blank stare. Confronted with a truth he'd been loathed to verbalize, an expletive spewed from his lips even as he heard his name.

"Chase…?" Ava's voice drifted like smoke towards him.

He couldn't respond to the truth of Poundsey's statement for Ava mounting the stairs, her gaze darting back and forth between the two men.

Her mouth hung open a moment before she was stalking down the hallway towards them. *"What in Hades?"*

Chase locked an arm about her waist, intercepting her advance. "Come on, baby—"

"No, you '*come on*' Chase!" She tried pushing him away, but he held fast. "I hear a rumpus and run up here hoping nothing's wrong with you, and find you fraternizing with a man I cut 'cause he put his hands on me?"

"Yeah…my apologies for that, Miss Ava," Poundsey began.

"'Miss Ava', my ass." She angrily shook her head. "Let go of me, Chase. I'm not doing this!"

"Doing what?"

"You wanna think twice before you insult my intelligence! *This*! Whatever it is."

Grabbing her hand, Chase turned towards his room. "Let's talk."

She snatched free of his grasp. "Let's not!" Her finger was a sword whipping in Poundsey's direction. "Not only is he the same clown running with that band of goons, but I saw you with my best friend at Brown's Ballroom. Lurlene Sims," Ava supplied at Poundsey's innocent look.

Chase endured the heat of her glare. "You wanna come with me, and let me talk to you?"

"*No, sir*! I'm packing my bags and getting wherever I'm going."

Eyes closed, Chase exhaled a frustrated breath, allowing her to get only so far ahead.

He caught her in the stairwell. Positioning himself in front of her, he managed to block her descent. "Ava, baby, come on. Calm down. Let's discuss this."

"Move, Chase. Stairs ain't no place to play."

"I'm in love with you, Ava, and you're not leaving this way."

There was a brief, but charged silence as his admission settled like sweet mist over them. The sweetness didn't prevent Chase from feeling the heat of her anger, or noting the pulsing of a vein in her neck.

"Word to the wise, Chase: honey, the Lord is my witness that I love you as well." She placed a hand on her chest. "With all of my heart I do. But that's not keeping me here."

"Sweetheart—"

"I've no idea what all you're involved in, but I ran outta Oklahoma, leaving a mess of nothingness and violence! I choose not to live that way never no more again."

His voice was low, edgy. "Ray Poundsey isn't a gangster. I employ him."

"For what? Fondling women? Let's forget him. Was my studio's vandalism related to *whatever* it is you do or don't do?"

Now in possession of the gold coin found on the premises by his clean-up crew, Chase was honest. "Yes." His stomach turned with acid at the sorrow possessing Ava's visage. He felt a 'goodbye' in the touch she lovingly laid against his face, an indescribable loss in the immense tenderness of her kiss.

Her eyes glistened with unshed tears when Ava whispered, "I came to California to pursue art and beauty, baby boy. I don't want ugliness." With that, Ava pushed past him.

He turned, watched the leaving of the only woman he'd ever love...

"Hell, no!"

Chase bolted down the stairs, catching up with her on the landing leading to her second floor room in sync with an ear-shattering, wall-shaking boom.

Chase grabbed Ava in time to keep her from tumbling. He held her tightly as sounds of unrest, and falling ceiling plaster settled around them. "Are you alright?"

Shaken and wide-eyed, she clung to him despite assuring him she was fine.

Snatching the firearm stashed at the back of his waistband, Chase shoved it into her hands when ushering Ava into her room. He had no idea what had exploded, or precisely where. He only knew an imminent threat had come too close for comfort. "Lock the door and stay here!" he ordered closing the door behind him. "*Poundsey!*" Not looking back, he could only pray for her safety as Chase descended the stairs two-by-two.

Fire was a hypnotic demolisher decorating the night. The heat of the flames feasting on Chase's truck was forcefully felt where he stood yards away mesmerized by the sight.

His momentary fixation was broken by the cries of alarm and worry around him. He snapped to attention, keeping Mz. Delsie and her lodgers exiting the house from getting too close to danger. In his periphery vision, Chase saw Ava atop the porch. She'd defied his instructions and joined the melee, clutching her robe about her—a horrified mask on her face.

Cursing her noncompliance, he left Mz. Delsie and boarders in Poundsey's care as he moved towards Ava only to hear what sounded like the too close rat-a-tat of gunfire. A quick glance over his shoulder provided a view of a black car rolling ominously towards them. In that moment he understand the detonation of his truck had been nothing but a ruse.

"Get down!" he bellowed as instinct took over, propelling his body forward despite being in the direct line of fire. He crashed into Ava, planting himself on top of her, bodily engulfing her in his protection until gunfire ceased and he felt danger pass.

Heart pounding, he elevated himself from her only to furiously check her person for possible injury. He sagged with relief when she assured him she was unscathed. The same couldn't be said of Chase. Blood trickled from his right shoulder where he'd been grazed by a bullet, sustaining a superficial wound.

"I'm okay," he repeatedly reassured above the sounds of Ava's desperate cries. Only the need to silence her fears kept him from indulging in a volatile need to pursue his assailants.

Holding Ava against him, Chase made quick work of ensuring everyone's wellbeing before herding Mz. Delsie and boarders back indoors. He issued orders, functioned proficiently and precisely, as if an automaton whose movements weren't wasted.

By the time the fire brigade extinguished the inferno, a disinterested police officer came and went, and Chase had managed to see the boardinghouse occupants as settled down for the night as they'd get, he was coiled tight with adrenalin.

Leaving Poundsey positioned on the first floor like a sentinel, he quickly climbed the stairs only for his heart to stop when nearing Ava's room. Finding it empty, Chase took off running. Calling her name, he raced to the third floor of the old Victorian. The relief he felt when seeing her outside his door was short-lived.

"*No.*" The guttural sound was both plea and command as he stared, heart dissolving in shreds, finding Ava with luggage and a folded note in hand. "Do. Not. Leave. Me."

Her voice was leaden, weak, her intent unmistakably clear. "Chase...it's too much..."

Though softly spoken, her words were knives that sliced. Severed in his soul, he reacted, grabbing her when she backed away as if what they had was loathsome. Her luggage fell unheeded as he maneuvered her into his chambers, kicking the door closed behind them.

Having lost but never loved, he was unmindful of his bandaged injury, embracing and kissing her with desperate abandon that conveyed his fear of existing without her. She responded with soft heat and gentle fierceness as he poured all he had into their loving. His every touch, kiss, nip, lick was layered and infinite—conveying the magnitude of his emotions and offered devotion. Chase loved Ava fierce, deep, complete. Like a libation, he poured into her his absolute everything.

Only when she slept soundly did Chase quietly ease from their shared bed. Watching her as he quickly dressed, he thanked God for another chance. To love. To cherish her. To give her the life she deserved. A life in which Ava was cared for and safe.

His jaw hardened thinking this house, and not his truck, could have been firebombed to hell. That hurt could have touched her. Unwilling to take chances with her future, her wellness or his, he secured his pistol at his ankle, another beneath his waistband, intent on collecting the rifle stored in a hidden panel of the grandfather clock downstairs. Tenderly kissing her forehead, he left the room determined that, tonight, this vicious game with Garamelli was done.

In the parlor, his brief conversation with Poundsey was followed by a telephone call during which Chase spoke two words only.

"Strap up."

The war was on. The gauntlet had fallen.

Three men lay massacred, bodies intact, expressions peaceful as if the rum they'd imbibed was heaven's best. Yet, Domino Garamelli and his goons lay in odd angles about the table, indisputably dead.

He stood in the doorway of Garamelli's hideout high in the Oakland Hills, assessing the scene, refusing to enter and sully himself with the murder of bastards who posed as men. Though their demise was less than two hours at best, the air was permeated with the stench of death, corruption, vileness and a familiar scent.

A sound in a corner caught his attention. His firearm was immediately aimed and lifted.

Quickly canvassing the dim space, Chase signaled his men before proceeding with stealthy silence towards the sound of weeping emanating from a corner of the room. Nearing the source, only a solid grip kept him from dropping his firearm.

"Marlon!"

His brother cringed against the wall, in a near fetal position, his face a factory of snot and tears.

"I did it, Chase. I fixed it!"

"Fixed what?" Chase reached down and yanked his brother to his feet when Marlon continued his nerve-wracking sobbing. An object fell from Marlon's hand in the process. Retrieving the object, he held a small bottle from which wafted the scent of garlic.

"It's Mother's arsenic. Like she puts on garden pests. I put it in the booze. I fixed it."

"Fixed what?" Chase roared.

"Sylas' death."

Time stilled.

"Chase, I swear, I didn't mean for it to happen! You told me to quit playing with passing. I didn't know who she was!"

Listening to his brother's emotional deluge, only God kept Chase from beating Marlon into an unrecognizable mess. Marlon had played with the color line at the cost of Sylas' life.

Playing white, Marlon engaged in an intimate relationship with a redhead who—unbeknownst to him—was part of Garamelli's personal stable of paramours. Currying Garamelli's favor, Marlon's pillow talk was stored and fed to Garamelli by the female.

"I laughed about Domino Garamelli stealing your shipment, then you stealing it back...and how Domino had been bested by Colored men." Marlon's shirtfront was sodden with tears. "Everybody thought Sylas was white, and the brains of the outfit. You were just the muscle. I told her folks had it wrong. Everything was opposite. The business was *yours*, that Sylas was just the front man. And that you were gonna strike one last time before easing out into your delivery business. *That's* what I did!" Marlon yelled, hitting his own chest. "That's why they killed Sylas! Not just 'cause y'all had the balls to take your stuff back, but because he was Colored! They knew that because of me, Chase! I opened my damn mouth one time too many!"

Eyes closed, Chase turned his face towards heaven. He and Sylas knew the risks they ran with his baby brother passing for the sake of their enterprise. A proud Colored man, Sylas used his skin color and ability to speak their father's French Creole solely when transacting business. His ability to semi-navigate French allowed them to negotiate for contraband shipments of liquor from Europe. The quality of the imported spirits being finer than the moonshine most Colored bootleggers had access to, in turn, increased their revenue. His white appearance enabled Sylas to bail Chase from jail whenever arrested—not for peddling liquor—but for selling to white establishments. Hearing that the absence of melanin had played into his brother's murder, Chase felt new rage towards his long-absent father. Yet, he stood rock-solid as Marlon—like a crumpled, deflated rag doll— sagged against him.

He let his brother weep until spent. "Who knows you're here?"

"No one."

"Marlon—"

"I swear to God, Chase, I didn't say nothing to no one! I got on that train to take Little Sylas to L.A., but decided to send Little Sy on home and got off earlier. I had to come back here and finish what I started."

"You could've gotten your fool self killed in the process!"

"Chase, I was careful. I swear! Garamelli didn't know me. He didn't know nothing about me being connected to you or Sylas."

Chase listened as Marlon explained flashing a roll of money at a card game a few nights back, and playing poorly on purpose.

"That's how I got in on tonight's set-up…and did what I needed to."

Chase looked around the room, noting the frozen tableau of dead men, dealt cards and chips atop the table. "I gotta get you outta here. You gotta disappear."

Marlon's weeping resumed. "I'm sorry, big brother."

"Yeah…maybe you are, Marlon, but you just made a mess bigger than I can fix."

"*No, I haven't!* Garamelli's in deep. He owes six-figures to a mob boss back east. That's what tonight was all about. He was tryna shave his debt, and only had another day to do it."

"You know this because?"

"The redhead Garamelli and I were both bed partners with."

"The same one who got our brother murdered by informing Domino that Sylas was a Colored man," Chase spat with open disgust.

Marlon looked away, chastened. "C.J., I did it for Sylas. I knew she had Garamelli's ear, so I…visited her to get what I needed. You see it worked! She told me what Domino didn't know: that mob boss from back east is already here and was coming for him. I just did him a favor and took out Garamelli before he could."

The pain of Sylas' death felt fresh as Chase stared at his one living brother. The solace in knowing Sylas' murderer had been dealt with was smaller than imagined. "Let's go."

He headed towards the entrance, pausing to flick two gold coins—one he'd kept since finding it a year ago near Sylas' body, and that found on the floor of Ava's salon—onto the table near Domino's dead hand. The coin spun, eventually settling into the pile of exact replicas already present.

He walked into the night, mindful that fate had intervened, swiping the need for vengeance from his grasp.

Dawn touched the horizon as Chase wearily mounted the stairs, the wound on his shoulder rhythmically throbbing.

Pausing outside his door, Chase leaned his head against it, accepting the gift of his life and his living rather than wishing the world wasn't what it was. His brother's murderer was dead, and Marlon was his murderer. Despite Marlon's story of a mob boss out for Garamelli's life, he couldn't take chances that Marlon's actions wouldn't come back to haunt them. He'd placed his brother on the Sunset Limited bound for New Orleans. Marlon could make it on his own or seek the aid of their father's relatives residing in the area.

It's up to him, Chase decided, quietly easing his bedroom door open. Guided only by the hand of dawn, he was careful to subdue excess noise and movement while sitting in a bedside chair to remove his shoes. He stopped midway, sensing an eerie stillness.

Jumping up, Chase turned on the lamp. His world crumbled in slow motion when finding the bed empty and Ava's luggage nowhere to be seen. His heart ripped in uneven pieces at the sight of her folded note on his pillow serving as a simple marker of what had been.

CHAPTER FOURTEEN
Ava
Three Months Later

Southern California's summer sun bathed her in bright light. Its delicious warmth, cast against her face, felt like days down-home. She basked in it, free of nostalgia, free of want. Rather, she sat—a handful of students clustered about her—in a field of wildflowers and the wonder of her world.

Thank You, Lord, for this living.

She'd run from precariousness and volatility only to land in an unlikely place of blessings. Grateful beyond belief, she was pleased despite life's imperfections and difficulties.

"Remember we're only sketching today. We paint tomorrow," she reminded her class, her mind's eye already capturing the colors tomorrow's lesson would allow.

Engrossed in their work, her students' "Yes, Miss Lydell" was effortless and automatic.

She smiled, satisfied by their focus and her instrumental role in helping develop their love of art.

Thank God this government's finally acting like we're human enough to deserve its help, she thought, still amazed that President Roosevelt and his New Deal had proven her patron.

In an effort to counter the dire impact of The Great Depression, the president and his cabinet initiated the Works Progress Administration. In its attempt to create employment for the vast spectrum of Americans, the W.P.A. allowed for the Federal Art Project, not as a cultural endeavor, but rather as a means of providing economic relief for varying artists by creating paid jobs and projects for which their services were enlisted.

Sculptors. Painters. Muralists, and more. Artists applied to the program in droves, finding relief for themselves and exposure for their work. Negro artists being allowed into the Federal Art Project was beyond astounding. Ava's literally learning of the program while fleeing heartbreak and an unstable situation had proven nothing short of miraculous.

"I'm finished, Miss Lydell!"

A student's gleeful declaration was a welcome deterrent keeping her thoughts from slipping into that quagmire of a pain-filled past that she preferred to sidestep.

"Let me see that masterpiece." Placing her own artboard on the grass beside her, Ava took the canvas from the child. Turning, examining it from every possible angle, she was forced to swallow a laugh and admit her inability to identify anything remotely artistic about it.

Lord, this looks like a bunch of rabid rats.

"Honey, your creativity is…unmatched," she praised. "I can't wait to see it when it's finished with all those pretty colors you like to add."

"But it don't look like yours, Miss Ava."

"Is it supposed to?"

"No, ma'am."

"One of the gifts the Good Lord gave us is having a unique and individual perspective. His world is too vast for us to be looking, seeing and acting the same. It's no different with this. You create from here." She pointed to the child's heart.

"Yes, ma'am, but next to your drawings mine looks like old alligators and eggs."

Her laughter danced across open space and warm air. "That's a bit extreme, baby. And like I've said before, in my class we don't rudely judge ourselves or our work 'cause it comes from love, and love is too colorful to be compared or contained." Returning the work to its creator, she glanced at her timepiece. "We're finished for the day. Time to clean up."

The groans and moans as students stopped their work and collected their supplies were easily replaced by youthful praise. It was Ava's rule: students were to examine each other's efforts and look for that which was discussion- or compliment-worthy.

Even if rabid rats are running across the page.

Smiling and tickled, she led the way across the field and back to the building housing the Pasadena Negro Art Center, the voices of her five students bouncing about her. While the center allotted designated space for her art lessons, she was known to change locations on a whim, taking students "out into the real world" in an effort to show them the often overlooked beauty hiding in plain sight of everyday life.

Washing up as her students stored their materials, Ava returned their goodbyes—watching each depart—before tidying the room in preparation for the next day.

"Miss Lydell."

Pausing her task, she glanced up to see the center's director at the doorway. Greeting him, Ava unconsciously, nervously fiddled with the front of the art apron draped over her neck, grateful for its over-sized roominess and large kangaroo pockets. She preferred her smock, but in the July heat it was too conspicuous.

"A parent's asking to enroll two children in your current class rather than waiting for the new session next fall as suggested. I know we have the space, but do you feel it prudent to start students three weeks into the program?"

"How about having them come in an hour early to do a project with me? That'll allow me to do an assessment."

Pleased by the idea, the director assured Ava the students' pre-paredness and admission to the program would be solely up to her judgment.

Appreciating his diplomacy, she already knew she'd admit the pro-spective students regardless of artistic ability. This government-spon-sored program was, in her opinion, a godsend that Colored children more than deserved. In addition to culturally enriching classes, freshly prepared lunches were provided daily, relieving many of the hunger waiting at home. She would turn none away.

Securing her supplies in her allotted cabinet, Ava ran a cleaning rag over various work surfaces, glad to do it. Teaching was energizing. Experiencing the wonders of art through the eyes of her students re-freshed her zest for life. The freedom to indulge in her own art before and after class, without worry for her well-being, was rejuvenating, cleansing. Daily, she felt her heart lean towards healing. Only nights proved a time for wrestling.

Finished with her clean-up, she said her good-night's before head-ing outdoors into the sweltering touch of the southern California sun. After life in the fog-laced cool of San Francisco, the heat felt divine.

Delicious...

Like a caress. A warm breath.

The fire in his kiss that she missed beyond reason...

She stopped in the middle of the block despite having eight more to walk.

Ava, girl, get your thoughts!

She'd come to accept being defenseless to want and whim, night after night being tormented when the day was done and there was nothing left to do, to occupy her mind or her time. In the solitary quiet of night, her tears flowed. Heartache rolled. Loneliness and memories flared so strongly that she felt him inhabiting the empty spaces of her bed and her body. But daylight had been her ally, whisking away her abject longing. Daylight gave her strength.

Rising with the sun, she painted prior to leaving for the Art Center where she proved a model worker, over-immersing herself in tasks both menial and meaningful. Arriving early, she stayed late. All in the name of escaping the tortuous absence of him. Her strategy had proven successful. Until recently. Now? She felt him as strongly by day as she did by night. Relief was no longer cradled in the warm arms and busyness of daytime.

Head lifted, heart set, Ava resumed the walk home. She couldn't afford the misery of memories. Her current predicament required level-headed focus.

Even without reading the note taped to her bedroom door, she knew its content.

Lurlene.

"That girl ain't nothing but relentless," she murmured, unfolding the missive and reading the message the housemother had left. Sighing, she tossed her pocketbook onto the narrow bed dominating her sparse room, and started to kick off her shoes. Having second thoughts, she headed for the parlor, electing not to avoid returning the call and a telephone conversation that obviously couldn't keep.

"Lurlene, let this be the last time we discuss this. It's my life and I'mma live it how I see fit."

"That man has a right to know where you are."

"Why? So I can warm his bed in between his running off to war?"

"Framing things up that way ain't hardly fair when you know that man ain't did nothing 'cept honor his family the way he saw fit."

Ava snickered mirthlessly. "Honey, what I know is I can't compete with that mistress." She would never regret loving Chase, or giving her whole self to him. If granted the opportunity, she would readily repeat their whirlwind affair completely and again. Loving him was like the vast colors of the sun setting on the ocean, or the deep rich of a midnight sky. Loving him beautified her soul, her life. That, however, didn't lessen the sting that even after his pleading with her not to leave, after filling her with the most profound intimacy she'd ever received, he'd left her alone in bed and walked into the seductive arms of his other lover. He was a man bent on vengeance. Violence was the mistress she couldn't best.

"All them little nappy-headed brothers and sisters you got, you telling me you wouldn't go after somebody for hurting one of 'em?"

"In a heartbeat. Let the Lord be my witness." Having learned the impetus of *his* actions from Lurlene, Ava was sympathetic yet unpersuaded. "But I know my limits, and bloodshed and all-out war is on the outside of 'em. Lurlene, I'mma love that man with my last breath, but I can't have all that havoc in my life. Especially now..."

"And what, exactly, you think he's gonna do when he finds out?"

"Lurlene Sims, if you open that mausoleum you call a mouth and say one word about—"

"Oh, hush up, gal! I ain't said nothing." Lurlene's sigh was nearly palpable. "But you know you gonna pay for keeping *that* from him."

"Maybe. But it's a worthwhile cost for doing right by me and mine. Now, either we talking 'bout something else or ending this phone call."

"Ava Lydell, you kin to ten donkeys and two mules."

Her laughter was welcome, refreshing. "So says you. How's Poundsey?" She noted the soft timbre of her friend's tone when Lurlene responded,

"Sweet as candy."

"Sounds like you wanna keep him."

"Sounds like that southern California sun done burnt your brain. Unlike you, I ain't never held myself to only one man. Think you'll ever come back this way? Or you staying down there even after...?"

A resounding knock interrupted Ava's response. Sliding the pocket doors open, the housemother stood at the parlor's threshold, her round face bearing its customary smile. "Ava, dear, you have a delivery. Mind if I have it sent to your room?"

"No, ma'am. Thank you," she responded, curious but electing to continue her phone conversation with Lurlene as the housemother closed the doors once more. Not having seen her friend since April, she missed her more than she let on. Flaws and all, Lurlene had always stood with her in times of crisis. Unorthodox though she was, she was still a blessing. She hadn't caved and disclosed Ava's where-abouts despite Chase's incessant requests, had even offered to accom-pany her on a train back to Oklahoma when the time demanded.

Lord, I can't go back.

Ava tried that arson-lit night that left her heart in pieces like shattered pottery. Riding the train from San Francisco, she'd disem-barked in Los Angeles in order to switch to a connecting route that would take her home to Oklahoma. Dismal thoughts of the vapid existence waiting down-home left her unable to take that second leg of her journey. Instead, feeling defeated and depleted, she'd retrieved her cardboard luggage and entered the adjoining coffee shop to cry solitary tears. Sick of herself and sorrow, she'd dried her eyes and ordered hot tea. As if too familiar with the plight of forlorn women, the waitress had served the tea along with a discarded newspaper and a pat on the hand.

"Reading about this crazy world might make whatever you're facing seem a little less bad."

Thankful for the touch of human kindness and something other than her own misery to occupy her thoughts, she'd readily indulged in a local newspaper three days past its circulation date. Reaching an article four pages in, she wanted to hug that waitress as if heaven-sent. There in black-and-white was information regarding the Work Prog-ress Administration's newly formed Federal Art Project. The sheer creation of such an endeavor was incredible, but the existence of the Pasadena Negro Art Center left her wide awake and praying despite the lateness of the night.

Funds nearly depleted when purchasing that train ticket home left her unable to afford accommodations. Instead, Ava hid in the train station until morning dawned, sponge bathed and changed her cloth-ing before spending what little she had left on carfare. Arriving at the Pasadena Negro Art Center, she inquired about employment only to learn of an art instructor position. Not having prior teaching experi-ence, she was thanked for her time, but denied. Desperate, she boldly grabbed a notepad and pencil from the director's desk. Sketching the portrait of her life, Ava offered it, leaving the director to sit in awe of his mirrored image staring back at him. Escorting her to the art room and offering her paints, he stood aside as she worked her magic. She left an hour later, employed with a weekly stipend and a room in the

Center's designated commune shared by three other resident instructors and presided over by a housemother.

Even now the joy of heaven's moving on her behalf was easily revisited. Yet, she couldn't escape a certain terror knowing that Colored folks' admission to the project was experimental at best.

"All Negro applicants must be above reproach, impeccable in decorum and moral condition…"

She'd signed an agreement. There were house visits, and impromptu drop-ins by a pinched-lipped, no-hipped, stern-faced white woman. As an agent of the Federal Art Project, it was her responsibility to ensure Negro participants "didn't shame the government and earned its faith" in them. That, and her housemates' responses to her constant decline of social invitations, were the flies in the ointment of her, otherwise, peaceful existence.

Kneading her eyebrows, Ava suppressed a sigh. She knew her fellow housemates thought her aloof, unwilling to socialize. She wasn't intentionally distant, rather protective. She stayed to herself in an attempt to—as long as possible—keep herself from suspicion and detection.

"Ava, it ain't nothing but a matter of time." Lurlene's voice brought her back to the conversation. The truth of her statement cut like a knife.

Wrapping her arms about her waist, she nodded as if her action was visible miles away. It was July: three months *since*. Time wasn't a friend in this.

Her volume was a near whisper. "I know, honey. Only thing I can do is get as much out of this as I can before I'm let go. Shame before God I got careless," Ava lamented, knowing an eviction from the program was inevitable, and that she'd be jobless and homeless. Again. "Girl, I'm too old to have acted plumb dumb."

"Honey, don't fault yourself. Fault all that hallelujah hiding in that man's pants."

"You ain't helping one bit, 'cept to make me laugh."

"Good. Time's too short to be walking 'round looking like you licking lemons…no matter how long or hard the road you walking. And like I said, when the time comes—whether you wanna be here, there, or even back home in Oklahoma with your family—we can walk that road together."

Mention of journeying long roads, reminded her how she'd come to love walking the streets of Pasadena with their sights and sounds of human traffic each evening. Tonight, she needed the streets and the opportunity to escape notions of her impropriety.

No matter how often she mentally revisited applications of down-home remedies, she failed to come up with anything amiss when doing so post-loving. Yet, obviously she had and was now confronted by a monumental mishap.

"It's monumental, but nobody's misfortune." Correcting herself, she headed to her small room intending to change into comfortable walking shoes.

"...impeccable in decorum and moral condition..."

The wording of the signed agreement felt like a torturous vise about her head.

Both her decorum and condition were questionable. She needed to make wise decisions before time and circumstance came calling. Other than those in her art community and the small church she often frequented, she knew few people in Pasadena. Going back to Oklahoma with its limitations, set-backs and sadness wasn't an option.

"I'd rather sip sour milk and eat green bread than go home and be a glorified mammy for some white family."

Opening her bedroom door, she decided northern California and Lurlene solely comprised her list of possibility. With a sigh, she determined she'd head back that way come fall; in time to—with God's help—find employment. And a midwife. The peace she felt with that simple plan and acceptance was suddenly sucked up in a vortex.

Wrapped in parcel paper, the item earlier delivered sat on a chest of drawers. Large and rectangular, the object was a distraction to the delicate and familiar fragrance wafting from a single, cream-colored rose placed at its base.

One hand bracing the wall, Ava sagged against it, shaking her head as if erasing the obvious.

Lord...no.

On unsteady legs, she backed from the room, retraced her steps. Frantically knocking on the housemother's private door, Ava lost sight of pleasantries when she answered. "Who delivered it?"

"Ava? Dear, you don't look well. What's the matter?"

"Please...who delivered that package?"

"I don't recall the name on the side of the truck, but a nice gentleman carried it to your room. Oh, Lord, nothing's missing from your room is it? I was there the whole time. I didn't see him bother nothing, and he seemed like a nice young man—"

"Describe him."

"Honey, you're starting to worry me."

"Please."

They exchanged a long, silent stare before the housemother complied. "He was tall, solid build, wide across the chest, young...well, young compared to me...maybe about my complexion. He wasn't wearing nothing remarkable, just denim overalls like most delivery men." The older woman paused as if mining memories for something significant. "Oh, and he was good-natured when I teased him about covering up too much of his good-looking with that hair on his face, that beard."

Ava's making it back to her room without crashing or collapsing was an accomplishment for which she couldn't take credit. Closing the door, she stood with her back pressed against it, staring at the rose as if willing it to disappear.

Only stubborn determination allowed her to move slowly towards the chest of drawers. Ignoring the rose and all its significance, she gave the large paper-wrapped parcel her attention. Slowly, carefully, she ripped the paper enclosing it.

Her heart skipped as precious colors peeked through torn paper fragments. Removing the wrapping in its entirety, she stood—a hand over her heart—enthralled by the one and only original work to survive the vandalism against her salon. She'd mourned its being left behind in her haste to the leave San Francisco. Now, there it was, in all its ethereal grace and glory.

Surely, Goodness and Mercy had followed her, no matter that she didn't want to be found.

She had no interest in his subtle suggestions and open flirtatiousness. She'd merely accepted the dance. Just as she'd merely gone through the motions of the next day, edgy and anxious.

Her students had noticed, muttering amongst themselves, unconvinced by her reassurances that all was well. When she'd left them outdoors, rushing to the Center's restroom, her ruse proved faulty. Only grace enabled her to complete the class, rather than dismissing her students unusually early.

Only a fool would be up here dancing with some stranger when you ain't been able to keep a thing down all day.

She was tempted to claim her intestinal woes were the result of whatever fool game Chase Jenkins was playing. But, her thickening middle and shrinking waistbands told another tale that—after her mother's multiple births—she knew all too well. She'd worked hard to conceal it from others, if not herself. Now, here she was, faced with the fact that the coconspirator of her condition was hiding here, somewhere, in the city. Unseen, but felt, just like their first night at Brown's Ballroom. Unlike that night, tonight she shared the company of a man for whom she felt absolutely nothing.

Shoulda stayed your hips at home.

Worn down by a day of uncommon agitation, she'd shocked her housemates by accepting their invitation to a night on the town. Her acceptance had been an act of defiance, a means of communicating that she *wasn't his*, as well as a welcome and wanted diversion. Now, Ava felt foolish for thinking she could escape the truth that there was only one *him*. Despite time, distance, and the unsavory situations loving him had subjected her to, her heart was still stuck and stolen.

Annoyed at her inability to divest herself of *his* hold, she backed away from her dance partner. "Thanks for the dance, honey, but I'mma need to sit myself down somewhere."

Unwilling to see her go, the man grabbed her hand. "We don't have to dance. How 'bout a drink?"

"That's sweet, but really, I'm on the verge of feeling ill."

A leering light lit his eyes. "I got ways to help you feel real good."

She patted his face. "The last man I let make me feel good left too much of himself in places another man ain't able to even touch or taste." With a smile, Ava walked away.

Gathering her drawstring evening bag from the table where they sat in the company of young men, she overrode her housemates' urging her to stay. Citing a headache, she said 'good night' and opted for the exit. Halfway there she was forced to make a sudden detour in search of the ladies' room. Feeling as if her belly had been turned upside down, she stood over the toilet dry-heaving, producing nothing. Still, she paused to rinse her mouth before rifling through her clutch for a stick of gum only to find the brown, gold-trimmed envelope instead.

With a sigh, Ava extracted the note that had been delivered to the Art Center accompanied by a single cream rose. She read it despite knowing every word written within.

> *I can't be with you in this, but I will love you for life.*
> *A.L.*

The folded farewell she'd left three months prior was now hers again, a newly penned message, like a rebuttal, scrawled across the bottom.

> *Life and love don't mean much without you in them.*
> *C.*

She refolded the note, sliding it back into its envelope, with slightly trembling hands. Her gaze was puzzled, intense as she stared at that brown envelope, finding in it something oddly familiar that she irritably and easily dismissed. Her thoughts were too consumed with how to resolve life's newest predicament to care about paper problems.

Exiting the restroom, she stopped at the coat-check counter long enough to request a cab. She needed to go home to sweet peace and a soothing bath.

Stepping outdoors, she was hit by a wall of heat despite the deep descent of evening. She was momentarily tempted to return indoors where fans cooled the front lobby.

The country woman in me likes all this heat. It helps me think.

As if burning away layers of uncertainty, she scanned the night sky and considered a life that felt fine for the first time in a long while. She worked. She went home. She lived privately, absent of mayhem and men. Now, her newfound well-being was at risk of being compromised.

You can leave and go somewhere else.

She exhaled a weary breath towards the star-kissed sky, recalling something he'd once said.

"A man who's right doesn't run."

Right versus wrong wasn't a deciding factor for Ava. Safety and serenity were.

Closing her eyes, she conceded that running wouldn't resolve a thing. He'd found her here despite her quiet living. He was out there, somewhere, biding his time. He'd come for what he wanted. The question was when?

She opened her eyes at the sound of an approaching vehicle. Its fine lines and darkened windows were far finer than anything offered by the cab company. Ignoring it, she scanned both sides of the street, hoping the requested car would arrive soon. Her feet ached and her belly was beginning to feel unsettled again.

"Miss Ava."

Her attention snapped towards a man exiting the driver's side of the now parked automobile.

Her eyes went round with recognition. "*Ray Poundsey?* Oh, Hades no, indeed! Stay your Colored tail away from me!"

She scowled at Poundsey's smiling like something was funny, as he stepped up to open the rear car door. Her vision was solely consumed by a carpet of cream-colored rose petals strewn about the car's interior, lending the night their exquisite scent.

Without a word, she took off walking.

"Miss Ava, you gonna get me killed!"

"You have my condolences. And give Chase Jenkins a message," she tossed over her shoulder, fixated on walking fast. "Tell him I'm never doing this with him!"

Escaping Poundsey and all foolishness, she rounded the corner only to freeze where she stood.

There curbside, another vehicle as equally fine as the first, waited. The man leaning against the passenger side, arms crossed over a wide chest, left her entire world utterly off-center.

More handsome than dreams recalled, finely suited, a fedora angled atop his head, Chase openly studied her. His hunger burning with molten intensity caused her to step backwards, intent on fleeing.

"Ava."

The gentleness of his tone conflicted with the predatory sleekness of his movements as he approached with unapologetic power and purpose.

Ava stood immobilized and breathless, her heartbeat the frenzied rhythm of hummingbird wings. Again, she stepped away, but not far enough to escape his reach. He was there obliterating her atmosphere, consuming her entirety.

She raised a halting hand, her only defense. Against Chase, it was useless.

"What are you never doing with me again?"

The deep waters of his voice rushed through her, smashing her defenses and leaving her weak. When Chase eased an arm about her and pulled her to him, claiming her mouth as his, Ava's resistance backslid.

CHAPTER FIFTEEN
Chase

His journey to that piece-of-a-town in Oklahoma and back had produced frustration and desperation, but no Ava. Leaving Poundsey to scour the Bay Area and its surrounding vicinities had proven equally dissatisfying. No matter Chase's best efforts and the exhausting of resources, his search proved fruitless. He was left questioning his sanity, feeling as if she was a mere vapor in wind. Only her profound impact and imprint resulting in his fractured and wounded soul assured him Ava Lydell had truly been.

In her absence, he vacillated between broken and bitter, ruthless and reckless. As weeks passed and he was faced with the agonizing reality of her absence, he became caged and restless, exacting his business with extreme vigor that left him exhausted. Then, like the calm after a storm, he was quiet. Silent. Left to face the consequences of life's actions. Sequestered in abject humility, he found himself repentant, seeking forgiveness. He'd played the role of a vengeful deity thirsting after retribution for his brother's death. He'd lost his remaining brother, and the only woman he was built to love in the process. Humbled, he pleaded with heaven and prayed to God on bended knee. *Most High, please bring her back to me.* Purged in soul, he was left with his seemingly unanswered prayer, and the silence of the Almighty. Now, months after the 'amen', she sat feet away, the beautiful intensity of her eyes digging deep beneath soul and bones. He'd spent months searching in vain only to find her near his home terrain, right under his nose.

After the too-long abstinence resulting from her absence, his deepest want was their sensuous reacquainting. Yet, he'd refrained from touching her since that searing curbside kiss. He could thank her not wanting to cause a public scene—as well as her realizing the futility of resistance—for her capitulating and coming with him. Her situating herself as far from him as possible during the ride here cautioned him to tread lightly and follow her lead. Loving would come. For now, he had to face her uncommon quiet so like a dormant volcano before erupting.

"Why're you here?"

Her irritation wasn't lost on him; even so, Ava's voice felt like long lost satin against his ears. His response was saturated with blatant longing. "Because I want you."

"Your wants ain't the same as my needs."

"Because I love you," he continued, undeterred by her irritability. "Because I'm a man needing not only you, but your pardon. I *never* intended for you to be put in precarious places you shouldn't've been, but I was fixed on fighting a fight to the finish because that's what I know to do. That's the way I've always lived." He paused, exhaling and wiping a hand down his face. "I've never been a fool, but I can stand to learn a thing or two. Wisdom says every battle has casualties. You go in praying for the best without knowing your losses or consequences in advance. You simply fight fixed on the win."

"And what exactly did you win in all this, Chase?"

He shook his head. "Not a damn thing, baby. Plain and simple, I lost my biggest loss of all."

His baritone was a low, slow rolling river as he told the tale in full. He laid his cards on the table, confiding in Ava every aspect of his rum-running. How he'd approached it as a means of controlling and defining his own output, and reaping income according to his own labor. "I was sick of doing the same, if not more work, but being paid less than a white man." Partnering with Sylas, their bootlegging was only to be a temporary enterprise and means to a desired end.

"I warned Sylas this U.S. government'll eventually get off its teetotaling intolerance and repeal Prohibition when they realize the revenue they could've made in taxes."

That philosophy in mind, Chase and his brother went in with a vengeance, tirelessly transacting business. They were efficient, quiet, striking like leopards at night. They kept their expenditures low, their profits high, amassing solvency for their family.

"It is what is. I did what I did. But the one thing I stayed away from was taking another man's life."

Others had no such qualms, and Sylas had died instead. Marlon's involvement aside, he would perpetually live with that loss on his heart.

"More than a year before Sylas died, we'd started pulling back and making plans to quit rum-running. We were both ready to walk away and, slowly but surely, we were."

"But it didn't walk away from you. It followed you to the Bay Area, baby."

"It didn't follow me, Love. I lured it."

Losing Sylas, he'd hijacked one of Garamelli's largest shipments in order to draw him to northern California where a final fight could be had away from the rest of the Jenkins clan. At the end of it all, Domino Garamelli was dead. Thankfully, Marlon's information had proven correct. Sylas' murderer had been in hock six-figures deep with the mob boss back east. When Garamelli's body was found, the boss—without the slightest remorse—celebrated by burning the place down, Garamelli's corpse in it. Even so, Chase demanded Marlon stay in hiding until told differently for his own safety's sake.

"I never thought Marlon would mess up by finishing a fight not meant for him. All I can say is God loves that boy something fierce and lets him land like a cat on its feet over and again. He'll be fine."

"Goodness and mercy..."

Chase nodded, pushing his shirtsleeves higher up his arms. "God's grace follows him every time." His baritone had remained smooth as honesty flowed. Now, conveying his largest loss, his voice faltered and caught. "You and me, however...has God's grace covered us? Can you love me again?"

When she didn't answer, he did what he came to do. Unstrapping the pistol holstered about his ankle, he emptied the bullets from its chamber onto a side table. Empty gun in hand, he moved to where she sat, intending to hunker down on his haunches, communicating through posture his heartfelt surrender. But Ava jumped from her seat as soon as he neared.

His eyes narrowed as he watched her move to the opposite side of the room, nervous energy radiating off of her in wide waves.

It was the same off-energy he'd felt when embracing her on that sidewalk. Her hunger had been too apparent for her not to return his ardent kiss. Yet, she'd anchored her hands on his midsection, pressing backwards, keeping their bodies from melding together the way he wanted.

Now, feeling her tension, slowly he sat in the chair she'd vacated, confused by her skittishness. He never had, never would use his size against her. Yet, she retreated as if fearing his nearness. Puzzled, he sat wide-legged while watching her move about the room, studying it, her back intentionally to him. More than the distance between them, something elusive scratched at the edges of his conscience. Unable to identify it, he carefully dismantled the pistol instead.

Placing its parts on the table centered between the two chairs, he spoke quietly. "I will always protect my family. Understand that. But this? It's finished. *I'm* finished."

When she glanced over her shoulder at the pieces of a firearm representing that which had separated them, he saw the fragility she couldn't hide. Her hurt became his.

He sat a moment with the weight of her pain before loosening his tie and unbuttoning his collar, needing relief and oxygen.

"Ava…"

She shook her head, indicating a reluctance to hear whatever would be said.

Gently, he proceeded, fervently praying that in her heart-of-hearts she wouldn't merely hear, but receive him. "I fault myself for every pain and problem I delivered to your doorstep. I take full responsibility, and ask your forgiveness." He paused, collecting himself and allowing her the opportunity to speak her peace. When she simply nodded, he continued in her silence. "I can't make up for what's been. I can only show you going forward that protecting and providing for you in a way that leaves you feeling safe and cherished is my first business."

His sense of relief when she ceased fingering the fireplace mantle to fully turn and face him was immense.

"Chase, I meant what I said. I will love you 'til I die. But I can't live wild. I gotta live right." Lifting a finger for each, she ticked off her grievances. "I can't do the goons…and guns, and all that other vile and violent messiness. The night fires, bootlegging and any other godforsaken follies…they're not for me. And hear me when I say the next fool to *ever* touch my art will wake up buried in the backyard."

He leaned forward, arms braced on his thighs. His voice was low, intentionally seducing Ava away from angst. "Understood. What else, baby? What ropes you need me jumping?"

"This ain't about making you jump or choose. I'm simply telling you what *I'm* unable and unwilling to do."

"What if I told you that for me this *is* about choice, Ava Lydell, and that I choose you? My word's my best bond, baby, and I'm telling you before God: I'm done with the past. Like I said, even before I loved you, I was making ways to leave that living."

"But you're still living off rum money," she countered, looking about his modest, but well-appointed, bungalow in what was swiftly becoming the Colored section of Baldwin Hills.

"Yes, ma'am, I am living off of what bootlegging allowed. And I won't insult you by claiming to the contrary. But I'm not burning it down or giving away what I worked hard for just to satisfy some need for moral atonement. I ran hooch. Illegally, and successfully. Plain and simple." He held up a silencing hand at her interjection. "Let me finish, please. Am I boasting?" He shook his head. "Not in the least. I lived what I lived, and I can't unwind that. But that's my past. You're my present."

His words lingered on air as they observed one another, surrounded by silence.

When venturing to speak, her voice was soft, tremulous. "You're not going back."

Relief rolled through him as Chase felt Ava's internal shift in her affirming versus questioning his intent. She had reopened herself to him. Beyond grateful, he offered honest assurance. "No, baby, I'm not. You have my word on that." Dividing his time between his investments in Sylla's Delivery Service, Brown's Ballroom, Miz Delsie's and two other properties recently acquired, he'd committed to making his way on honest earnings. Removing a loaded money clip from his pocket, he tossed it on top of the dismantled gun parts and shrugged. "Quiet as it's kept, I've made nothing but clean money these last nine months."

He might have missed the way she flinched at the final two words of his statement had he not been regarding her like life depended on it. Experiencing a tightening in his chest, he continued in a slightly distracted manner. "Sylla's Delivery Service is taxpaying and law-abiding. I plan to expand and have Poundsey—"

"Is that how you found me? Through Poundsey, courtesy of that loose-lipped Lurlene?"

He didn't bother denying her correct summation. Neither did he relay Lurlene's refusal to reveal her precise whereabouts. Or that she'd sent him searching for a needle in a haystack with her cryptic, "Look for some Colored art centers down there. Find one, you might find Ava." His head cocked to the side, he was far too arrested by his steady perusal of her person.

His focus was fixed, penetrating and deliberate, missing nothing. His gaze slowly roamed her face, the full swell of her breasts. He felt an odd quickening when noting the slight thickening of her once narrow waist. The added flare of her already healthy hips that her fashionably designed dress—with its dropped waist and gentle folds—failed to conceal. Barely aware of her agitated complaints over Lurlene's betrayal, his eyes shot back to her midsection. The elusive thing that had plagued him since stepping away from that car and taking her in his arms was there, hidden in plain view.

As if icy water had been tossed into his face, Chase sat ramrod straight and stock-still.

"...I guess the housemother told you my whereabouts tonight. After Lurlene, charming her must've come easy..."

Her voice fading when noting his targeted scrutiny, their eyes met and held. A sharp current of energy passed between them.

In one fluid movement, he stood and crossed the room, making space nonexistent. He saw panic flit across her face as she took an involuntary step backwards while wrapping arms about her middle as if cold, protective. This woman was his one and only want, and he'd lived these past months craving her until every muscle in his body ached. Yet, he paused, curtailing urgency, before touching her gently. Cupping her face, he delighted in her softness.

"Ava?"

She would have turned away but for his snaking an arm about her waist. Gently cradling her chin, he angled her face towards him only to find her vulnerability on full display. "What're you hiding?"

Her increased inhalations mirrored his own rapid respiration as his emotions arced wide in their range from relief to thankfulness at her presence, to the wild swirling in his gut that demanded answers. He whispered in her ear with heightened urgency. "Tell me."

Eyes flooding with tears, she merely stared up at him as if willing him to take their worlds and make them right again.

Eyes locked on hers, Chase allowed his hands to seek their own answers. Gliding over her body, his touch was tender yet hungry as he re-familiarized himself with the midnight silk of her skin, every generous curve and endowment. Feeling her tense when he reached her middle, he cradled her firmly against him, perceiving differences, his eyes narrow with suspicion.

"Chase..."

"Shhh," he quietly soothed, gently turning Ava in his arms so that he stood behind her as they both confronted a dressing mirror. With unapologetic intent, he unzipped her dress and unfastened her brassiere, sliding both from her body in a deliberate unveiling. Unable not to, she leaned back into his embrace as he tenderly cupped her heavier breasts before sliding his hands to reverently cover the soft, nearly imperceptible round mound her belly created.

Chase's voice was raw, strained. "Are you carrying my child?" Gaze affixed to her mirrored image, he watched her tears spill. "Ava?" he insisted at her silence.

Breath trapped in his chest, he audibly exhaled when she nodded.

Defenseless to a sudden hurricane of emotions slamming into him, Chase bowed his head. Struggling with oxygen, he forced himself to breathe calmly until in control of himself once again.

Feeling her palm against his face, he lifted his head. Tears pouring, her voice was thin and choked. "Deception wasn't never what I wanted. Forgive me. *Please.*"

His spirit resonated joy and peace at her humble confession and apology.

"Honey, I left for me. But when I realized…I stayed gone…to keep our child outta harm's way."

A flicker of anger came and weent. He consumed her mirrored allure, inwardly conceding that her protective act may have been part of God's plan. While their estrangement had been unwelcomed and unwanted, heaven had used it to shape and tone him into that which was fit for their future.

I'm a better man.

He kissed her palm cradling his face. The simple act granted forgiveness.

"This is my child." He touched her with awe, his hands sliding over the generous curves he loved and wanted, only to return to her belly and the newness of life nestled within.

"This is," she softly affirmed, covering his hands with her own before turning to kiss him.

After unwanted months of absence and abstinence, her touch and taste were tortuous. Her fingers unbuttoning his shirt and lovingly stroking the fully healed bullet wound on his shoulder heightened his torment. Her slowly licking his lips had his hunger rising with a vengeance. Still, he managed to not be derailed even while backing her towards his bed. Thoroughly immersed in her kiss, one arm about her, he fumbled in the bedside table drawer until grasping what he needed.

With concentrated gentleness, he inclined her backwards until prone across his bed. Standing between her legs, he bent to kiss her belly before placing an oval-shaped box atop its soft firmness.

He watched as, brows furrowed, she elevated onto her elbows to see the waiting gift. His lips curved in a grin when her eyes widened.

"*Chase*...honey...what is this?"

Defying his nervousness, he knelt before opening the box to display the dazzling emerald-cut diamond inside. "Marry me."

Gripping the box, she eased into an upright position, wide-mouthed and tongue-tied.

"You love me, woman?" he asked when she'd sat too long without a response.

Cupping his face, she answered honestly. "Like I never will another man."

Without hesitation, he slid the ring onto her finger. "Then marry me. I need you. I need my child."

"We need you, too, Mr. Chase Jenkins," she purred against his lips before sweetly kissing him. "You love me back, baby boy?"

"Woman, you already know this."

"About how much?"

A wicked, ravenous gleam in his eyes, he maintained his kneeling position while gripping her hips and pulling her towards him. Eyes locked on hers, he gently stroked her breasts. Slowly, wantonly he reacquainted himself with their deliciousness. Laving, licking, he learned their newness. Her heat and her want were immediate, her breathing rapid as sounds of pleasure sprinkled from her lips. Delighting in the sweet clean of her fragrance, he defied his own extreme need to be fully buried, moving in her warm, silky depths. Rather, he kissed a hot, tender trail down her hungry flesh. "To play on the wise words of the woman I love..." He paused to drape her legs over his shoulders and incline her flat against the bed. His grin was devilish as he reverently kissed her belly and blew warm breath. "Sweet Thing, I can taste you better than I can tell."

CHAPTER SIXTEEN
Mr. & Mrs. Jenkins

Eight days later, before a minister, vows were simply said, every word a beacon of devotion and light bright enough to last a lifetime.

From the culinary spread to the unsolicited advice Chase's older female relatives freely gave, Ava was engulfed by the ready love of the Jenkins clan. That love lessened the blow of her father's refusal to attend their nuptials. Still bitter over her "walking out" in pursuit of her own happiness, her father had remained in Oklahoma while her mother and Ava's four oldest siblings accepted Chase's providing train tickets for them to attend. In the presence of family and friends, their humble ceremony had been magnificent. When the festivities ended and the newlyweds returned to their Baldwin Hills home further beautified by her recently created art, she felt as if she were descending from a day spent amid clouds.

"Little Sylas was the sweetest ring bearer this side of the Delta."

"Yeah." Chase laughed, gripping her hips and carefully guiding his blindfolded wife. "That cat's cute and he knows it. But I'll tell you something. He looked just like my brother all suited up like he was."

"Did you really feel Sylas' presence during the ceremony?"

He nodded as if his wife could see him. "Sylas' spirit definitely made an appearance."

"Too bad Marlon didn't."

Opening the door to the room at the back of the bungalow, he admitted, "We won't be seeing my brother anytime soon, and not because of the mess he made murdering gangsters. Relatives down-home say Marlon's fully walking on the white side."

"Honey, no!" Incredulous, Ava stopped and fiddled with her blindfold. "Marlon's passing full-time?"

"Woman, leave that handkerchief where it is," he playfully scolded. "And, yeah, Marlon's playing white down there in New Orleans. But, I know my brother. He'll be back when he needs something, or when he sees that being a colorless man isn't everything he thinks it is."

Ava clutched her husband's hands planted about her hips. "Chase Jenkins, you better not bump me into nothing." She smiled when he laughed despite the tragedy of losing a brother to that abyss caused by racism. "Lord, that Marlon mess is enough to make me sad; but I'll tell you what I'm finding sweet."

"Me?"

"Like butterscotch and honey. But I was talking 'bout Lurlene and Ray Poundsey."

"Do not move," Chase instructed, leaving Ava long enough to turn on a lamp in the glass-enclosed sunroom.

"You think Ray knows about Lurlene's...*activities?*"

"A man knows his woman," was his absentminded reply. "Not one of us has lived sin-free. Lurlene's good people, and as long as she's good to Poundsey we have no problems."

"I can't believe Ray's headed back Up North with Lurlene to run Sylla's Delivery Service there while you head the business from here. You think he'll be satisfied even though the earnings might not be as much as y'all made rum-running?"

He laughed. "It's honest living, baby, and Ray'll do well. Even if he doesn't turn as pretty a penny, Lurlene's plenty incentive to keep Poundsey in place. Alright. You ready, Ava Lynne Jenkins?"

She smiled brightly. "Yes, sir, I am." Ava rapidly blinked as Chase removed her blindfold, allowing her eyes to readjust to the light. Covering her mouth, she squealed her delight when seeing what lay before them.

A large easel was surrounded by four miniature versions of itself. Stools. Tables and supplies. Canvases and smocks. A beautifully etched sign bearing Art by Ava, and in a far corner a pottery wheel. The sunroom had been transformed into a studio with classroom capabilities. After being evicted as an artist-in-residence because of her pending marriage and "expectant condition", he'd taken great pains to ensure there were no deterrents to his wife's dreams.

"Chase Edward Jenkins!"

He inhaled deeply, praying their last argument on the matter of his providing for her had truly been their last.

The night of their engagement—after a sensuous reunion that left them mutually useless—she'd placed her ring box in the bedside table drawer only to find several gold-trimmed, brown envelopes there. Remembering first sight of them, she'd finally put two and two together and rightly concluded his being the patron who'd once paid her landlord six months' rent on her San Francisco studio.

Sedated by good loving, she hadn't objected with her usual vehemence. Yet, she'd bristled a bit at being a "kept woman."

Drowsy and sated, he'd replied between yawns, his voice low but firm. "If I wanna take care of you, I sure as hell will. 'Cause I sure as hell can. Giving Randolph that rent was one thing I could do exclusively for you, to make sure—no matter what became of us—you'd be okay. When a man loves a woman he wants her well. I'm not some miscellaneous Negro running in and out your life without caring about your welfare. I'm yours, and I take care of mine. Now deal with that, Miss Ava Lydell, without expecting me to apologize."

Her lack of a comeback had surprised him then, just as her flinging her arms about his neck and kissing him profusely did now. "Thank you, thank you, *thank you*, baby."

"I figure you can paint for yourself, teach, whatever strokes your fancy," he answered, his eager hands slowly stroking and kneading her hips.

"You are too good to me!"

"You ready to reward me?" he asked, fingering the floor-length negligee hugging Ava's increased curves like a caress.

"Maybe."

"Maybe nothing, woman. We made a deal."

"Well, I'm reneging. I am *not* doing that with you."

"You gotta give to get, Mrs. Jenkins."

"I should've never told you what I did."

Drawing his wife to him, Chase chuckled mischievously. "What? That you've wanted to paint me in the nude since the day we met?"

Stroking his face, she purred seductively. "You gonna use it against me at every opportunity?"

"Hell, yeah and yes, ma'am. You wanna paint me in all my glory?" He trailed a finger down her cleavage. "I'm putting sweet potato pie wherever, however I choose."

Ava licked her husband's lips. "You ain't right."

Careful of her belly, he bent, scooping her over his shoulder. Peals of laughter poured from her throat as he exited the sunroom. "I'm not tryna be right. I'm tryna make it memorable, my tasting you as my wife for the first time."

"Fine! But only once, baby, and no more, never again."

Resituating her in his arms, her embrace about his neck, Chase merely grinned.

"I'm not playing," Ava insisted, smoothing a hand over the deep waves of his hair and smiling despite his mischief.

"Neither am I," he taunted, deeply kissing the love of his life as he carried her to their marriage bed covered in creamy roses. His kiss deepened thinking on the slice of sweet potato pie waiting on the nightstand—a slice he intended to strategically place and slowly eat like a grown, damn-done-in-love, married man.

Next in the Decades Series:

Warner Hughes returns home from war with the lingering effects of battle. Abandoned by his sweetheart and ostracized by his community, he feels he has no real home.

Elizabeth "Betty" Daniels has one love: music. Betty's family wants to see her married, busy with affairs of the home, leaving no time to pursue her art.

Warner's only solace is in the sweet melody of Betty's music. To Betty's mind, marriage means giving up the freedom to pursue her art. Can Warner let love in, and can Betty make room for love?

SUGGESTED DISCUSSION QUESTIONS
For Book Clubs and Reading Groups

1. How would you describe Ava's character?
2. How would you describe Chase's character?
3. What attributes were most appealing to you about our heroine and hero? What characteristics were annoying?
4. What circumstances prompted Ava to leave Oklahoma?
5. Did you, or family, migrate from the south in search of opportunities elsewhere?
6. Why did Ava leave Harlem instead of fighting to make a living there?
7. Provide examples of how racism appears "out west" and hampers Ava's life.
8. Why did Chase elect to become a bootlegger?
9. If *The Art of Love* was set in contemporary times, what do you think Chase's profession would be?
10. How does Chase's profession affect Ava's attraction to him?
11. What led to Ava's homelessness and how does she manage it?
12. Can you name the title of another book also written by this author that's mentioned in *The Art of Love*?
13. Ava's grandmother was lynched for preaching civil rights and against liquor. Was it surprising to know that, historically, women and not just men, were often the victims of lynching?
14. How did life harden both Ava and Chase to love?
15. Ava is four years older than Chase. Have you ever been involved in a romantic relationship with someone younger than you? If no, would you?
16. What do you make of Lurlene and her profession? Why was prostitution often engaged in by African American women during this era?
17. What did you like most about Chase and Ava's love affair?
18. In what ways does colorism impact Ava's life?
19. Despite being born and raised in poverty, Ava's an extremely proud woman. How does this pride hinder her? How does it help?

20. In what ways does the phenomenon of "passing" impact our characters' lives?

21. In your opinion, was Chase right or wrong for seeking retribution for Sylas' death?

22. If you could paint the future, where do you see Chase and Ava five years after *The Art of Love* ends?

ACKNOWLEDGEMENTS

I couldn't acknowledge anyone here if I couldn't write. And I couldn't write without the Lord. Thank You Abba Father for doing what You've done and what You do. I'm excited to see what's to come. I love You to life!

My husband who takes care of me, keeps me sane, and provides the tenderness in every hero I write: you are that man.

To my children who smile and hug me even though I'm so not lit or cool: you are my heartbeat.

To my mother, sisters, nephews, & great niece I give my appreciation and affection.

To my Club N.E.O. sisters (Anita, Joy, Sheryl, Twinny-Twin, & Tiffani): thank you for your unswerving support.

To my sisters & one brother in Salon Suzette: you keep a sister rocking and wanting to write. Thank you!

To my beloveds who constantly encourage and support me: we did it again! Thank you!

POETIC LICENSE

The author fully acknowledges that the Work Progress Administration (later named the Work Projects Administration) was created in 1935, two years after Prohibition ended. It's creation of the Federal Arts Project was too good a boon to Ava's story to pass up. Thus, the author took creative license in including it in *The Art of Love*.

WONDERFUL READERS...

Thank you for being the backbone of the literary community. Without your support, writers' works would collect dust and go unnoticed. So, I thank you for noticing me!

I have a secret to share: I absolutely *love* hearing from and interacting with readers and book clubs in person or via Skype and Facetime. Let's connect via any of the following:

EMAIL: sdhbooks@gmail.com
FACEBOOK: Suzette Harrison or Suzette D. Harrison Books
GOODREADS: Suzette D. Harrison
INSTAGRAM: suzetteharrison2200
NEWSLETTER SIGN-UP: www.sdhbooks.com
PINTEREST: Suzette D. Harrison Books
TWITTER: @Ariasu62
WEBSITE: www.sdhbooks.com
YOUTUBE: Suzette Harrison

If you enjoyed *The Art of Love* I'd be honored if you'd share that enjoyment by posting a review on Amazon.com and/or other venues such as Goodreads. If you're using a Kindle, the app lets you post a review when finishing the book. How cool and convenient is that? So, please take a brief minute to share your perspective. Your review can be as brief as a sentence, but it has tremendous impact. And by all means, please tell a friend!

Thank you for joining my journey! Until next time...

Blessings & peace,
Suzette

ABOUT THE AUTHOR

Suzette D. Harrison, a native Californian and the middle of three daughters, grew up in a home where reading was required, not requested. Her literary "career" began in junior high school with the publishing of her poetry. While Mrs. Harrison pays homage to Alex Haley, Gloria Naylor, Alice Walker, Langston Hughes, and Toni Morrison as legends who inspired her creativity, it was Dr. Maya Angelou's *I Know Why the Caged Bird Sings* that unleashed her writing. The award-winning author of *Taffy* is a wife and mother who holds a culinary degree in Pastry & Baking. Mrs. Harrison is currently cooking up her next novel...in between batches of cupcakes.